How *dared* he lecture her on what she should do and what she shouldn't?

"Being a mother as well as the sole breadwinner does carry certain responsibilities," Kay said testily. "Not that you'd know anything about that, of course. We can't all please ourselves and burn the candle at both ends."

"You don't even get a light near the wick," Mitchell said relentlessly, rising to his feet and placing his empty glass on the mantelpiece before walking over to her. "Come here," he said very softly, stopping just in front of her chair and holding out his hand to pull her up.

Her panicky heartbeat caused her breathing to become quick and shallow, but she managed to sound reasonably firm when she said, "No."

He bent down, taking her half-full glass from her nerveless fingers and placing it on a small table at the side of the chair. She stared up at him, her eyes deep brown pools. He was going to kiss her again, and it was only in this very instant that she admitted to herself how much she wanted him to.

Anything can happen behind closed doors!

Do you dare to find out…?

Welcome again to DO NOT DISTURB!

Mitchell Grey is a confirmed bachelor with
a painful past. But that is until he meets
single mom and successful business owner
Kay Sherwood. Drawn together, they soon
realize that they cannot resist the passion that
flares between them—and they discover that
they definitely *don't* want to be disturbed!

Join Presents® author Helen Brooks on a
yuletide journey to love, one that you
will not want to put down.

So what happens when Kay allows herself
to succumb to her desire for Mitchell?

Turn the pages and find out!

Helen Brooks

THE CHRISTMAS MARRIAGE MISSION

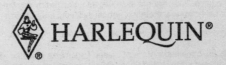

TORONTO • NEW YORK • LONDON
AMSTERDAM • PARIS • SYDNEY • HAMBURG
STOCKHOLM • ATHENS • TOKYO • MILAN • MADRID
PRAGUE • WARSAW • BUDAPEST • AUCKLAND

ISBN 0-373-12436-8

THE CHRISTMAS MARRIAGE MISSION

First North American Publication 2004.

Copyright © 2003 by Helen Brooks.

www.eHarlequin.com

Printed in U.S.A.

CHAPTER ONE

THE offices were lush, very lush—all muted tones of ochre and buttery yellows on pale maple flooring, and, although Kay could sense a discreet urgency behind the glass doors she was passing on her way to the big chief's domain, the overall air of tranquillity was not disturbed. The glass lift that had transported her from the thickly carpeted reception to the fifth floor had been the last word in elegance too.

She knocked on the door with the nameplate reading 'Miss Jenna Wright, Mr Grey's secretary', and waited until the woman inside raised her head from the word processor in front of her before opening it. Nevertheless, the beautiful cold face in front of Kay did not return her smile, and such was the expression in the carefully made up green eyes that Kay found herself speaking coolly as she said, 'I've a package for Mr Grey. I understand it is urgent.'

Still the woman did not smile or speak, merely holding out her hand for the large manila envelope with an imperiousness that was insulting all by itself.

Mr Grey's secretary obviously thought it beneath her to speak to a humble delivery agent, Kay thought wryly, aware that the woman's gaze had taken in every crease and mark on her biking jacket and leathers. She walked across to the large desk and placed the envelope in the red-taloned hand waiting for it, and it was only then the thin, scarlet-painted mouth opened briefly to say, 'Wait outside until Mr Grey has looked at it.'

Charming. Kay turned abruptly, aware her cheeks were flushing, and left the office without another word. She stood quietly for a second in the corridor outside, willing the colour in her cheeks to subside before she was forced to speak to the other woman again, and then walked over to where an area was set aside for visitors. Seating herself on one of the big plump sofas, she reached for a glossy magazine. When Mr Grey's secretary wanted her—and she had already been told by the firm who had hired her to take the documents to Grey Cargo International there would be a reply—she could jolly well come and find her!

In spite of her irritation, as the minutes ticked by Kay found herself engrossed in the story of a massively fat woman who had decided to have her stomach stapled. The article chronicled the highs and lows of the woman's two-year fight to become the size twelve she'd been before her husband had left her after their two children had died in an accident. Kay was so taken up with the battle that she found herself grinning like a Cheshire cat when the 'after' picture showed a slim, confident, smiling woman on the arm of a new man, and she was just muttering what she would have liked to have done to the first husband who had deserted his wife when she'd needed him the most—thereby contributing to the eating disorder she'd developed—when she became aware she wasn't alone.

She raised defensive brown eyes, expecting to see the perfectly coiffured figure of the secretary in front of her, and then froze for a second as an amused smoky voice said, 'Interesting?'

The man was tall, six feet two at least, and aggressively handsome in a hard, cold way, his silver-blue eyes and black hair holding no signs of softness or warmth, and his lean, powerful body intimidating.

'I...I'm sorry?' It was all she could manage through the wave of shock that had her rooted to the seat.

'The magazine.' He gestured at it almost impatiently. 'Is it the latest fashion, or a new hairdo which is so riveting?'

The condescension was so overtly patronising that it worked like an injection of adrenalin. Kay jumped to her feet, pushing back her mass of thick curly red-brown hair, which always exploded into riotous disarray every time she took off her crash helmet—and which she had long since given up trying to control—and took a deep breath. 'Neither,' she said icily. 'Just an article which reaffirms what swines men are, actually, although perhaps that's not very fair on pigs.'

He blinked. 'Right.' There was a brief pause and she noted with some satisfaction that both the amusement and condescension had vanished when he said coldly, 'You are the courier, I take it?'

Well, it was better than delivery girl, which she was sure was how the secretary would have referred to her. Kay nodded. 'Yes, I am,' she said coolly, her heart beginning to thump harder as it dawned on her this must be Mitchell Grey himself.

He said nothing for a moment, but then he didn't have to—the arctic eyes said it all. Kay was well aware that at a slender five feet five she wasn't the average courier, but, as her firm dealt only with the delivery of documents, letters and small packages, brawn didn't come into it. Her ancient but trustworthy 100 cc motorbike could nip through the traffic jams that sometimes snarled up Romford town centre, which was all she asked of it.

'How long have you worked for Sherwood Delivery?' The words themselves were innocuous enough; his tone suggested the firm must have been crazy to take her on.

It was therefore with a great deal of inward pleasure, none of which was betrayed in her cool voice and blank face, that Kay said, 'Ever since I formed the company three years ago.'

He didn't blink this time, which said a lot for his self-control, Kay had to admit, but she just *knew* she had surprised him again, even though his face was deadpan. He continued to watch her steadily, the silver-hued eyes narrowing, before he walked across to where she was now standing.

Kay was immediately aware of feeling dwarfed, which in the circumstances was not pleasant, but she instinctively raised her small chin as she waited for his response.

'Sit down, Miss...?'

'Sherwood. *Mrs* Sherwood.' And game, set and match to me, I think, Kay thought delightedly. It might teach him not to make so many high-handed assumptions in the future at least?

She saw him glance at her ringless hands as she took the seat she had just vacated, but as she watched him seat himself opposite the sofa she made no attempt to explain further. It was none of his business.

'Three years.' He sat back, one ankle resting on the other knee in a very masculine pose. 'Why haven't I heard of your company before this?'

Keep calm and don't gabble, Kay warned herself silently. He was no doubt well aware of the faintly menacing air he gave off and probably well versed in the art of subtle—and not so subtle—intimidation. But he didn't frighten her, not for a minute!

'Probably because we are still very small,' she said evenly. 'We deal with files, documents, letters, photographs—that kind of thing.' She knew it had been an urgent document she had delivered to him today from a firm of solicitors in the town, a document that needed a signature, but that was all she had been told.

'Your husband is a partner in the company?' he enquired softly.

'No.' It had been all the explanation she'd been going to give but, when the silence stretched and lengthened unbearably, she found herself saying stiffly, 'I'm divorced. I founded the company after we'd parted; he was never involved with it.' She glanced at the envelope in his hand, her voice dismissive when she said, 'If the document is ready, I'll take it now, shall I? I understand it's urgent.'

He didn't reply to this. What he did say—the cool, smoky voice deep and low—was, 'I would like to be able to understand how you got started, Mrs Sherwood. Small business ventures are fascinating, don't you think? What prompted you to choose such an...unusual career move?'

Career move? Kay stared at him, her big brown eyes betraying none of the whirling confusion in her head. Not so much a career move as survival.

For a moment she was tempted to spring up, grab the letter and make a dash for it, but common sense prevailed. She didn't like his cold contemplation one bit, and sitting here in these lavish, grand offices in her old scuffed leathers opposite a man who looked as if he was clothed by Armani at the very least, was not her idea of fun. But insignificant as he made her feel, she wasn't going to give him the satisfaction of thinking he had unnerved her.

She resisted the impulse to fiddle with her hair, deeply regretting that she hadn't taken the time to pull it back into a pony-tail as she normally did when she removed her helmet, and marshalled her racing thoughts. The bare outline, that was all he needed to hear. Nothing personal.

And then he completely threw her off balance just as

she was about to begin when he said, 'How old are you, anyway, if it isn't a rude question?'

It was. *Very* rude, in Kay's opinion. Resentment darkened the brown of her eyes to ebony, but she managed to keep her voice under control when she said crisply, 'I am twenty-six,' her tone adding silently, Not that it's any of your business.

The carved lips twitched a little. 'You don't look a day over eighteen.'

If she had a pound for every time she'd been told how young she looked she would never need to work again, Kay thought irritably. And she hated having it drummed home. Unfortunately her elfin features combined with a liberal dusting of freckles across her nose contributed to the overall image of a teenager, and when she tried to remedy the situation she always ended up looking like a little girl playing at dressing up.

She reminded herself that the customer was always right—although in her experience they rarely were—and took a deep breath. 'You asked how I got started,' she reminded him evenly. 'It was almost by chance, actually. I was asked to pop a letter in to someone as a favour one day; the sender knew I lived in the same street and the letter was urgent.'

He interrupted her, asking smoothly, 'Who was the sender?'

'My boss.' It was meant to be succinct.

'And you were working for...?' He had ignored her tone.

'A small accountant's.' And she'd hated every minute, loathed it, but it had been a job and she had needed one desperately. Having left university with a degree in Business Studies, she'd felt she ought to put it to use but from the first day had felt like a square peg in a round hole.

'Anyway,' she continued, trying to ignore the intent gaze, 'I started to think a bit. I knew there was always the Post Office and the railway, to say nothing of special services and so on, but when I made a few enquiries I found that lots of companies sent urgent messages—files, documents and so on—by taxi or by means of a large company car. Sometimes a Rover car or something equivalent with a chauffeur would travel twenty miles for one letter. I'm cheaper and faster.'

''I'm sure you are, Mrs Sherwood.' It was very dry.

Kay continued to look somewhere over his left shoulder as she went on, 'I drafted and designed a leaflet and a local printer ran it for me—'

'What did it say?'

She did look at him then—she hated being interrupted and twice in as many minutes had 'the customer is always right' scenario flying out of the window. He was gazing at her quizzically, his big body lazy and relaxed and his arms draped either side of the back of the sofa, and the sharp words she had been about to voice died in her throat as sheer sexual magnetism hit her like a bolt of lightning.

There was a small—and for Kay—fraught silence before she managed to pull herself together and say quickly, 'Something along the lines that we could give fast, direct, door-to-door service for delivery of documents and letters etc. anywhere in the Romford area. Same-day service guaranteed and to phone for immediate attention.'

'We?'

'My brother was out of work at the time and he was available to man the phone and see if my idea worked. It did, so within two months I'd given my notice and joined him. We started off with just the motorbike—' she indicated her leathers '—but now we have two vans and one of my brother's friends works for us. We have our own office in town since last year and so much work we're thinking of taking on someone else.'

He sat up straight, the movement causing a response in Kay she could well have done without. 'Impressive.' He nodded slowly. 'Have you a business card?'

'Sure.' She had flushed scarlet but she couldn't help it—the red hair went hand in hand with a porcelain skin that was prone to blushing. She fumbled in her leathers and brought out one of their neat little cards, handing it to him as they both rose to their feet.

'I mustn't keep you any longer.' He passed her the manila envelope, suddenly dismissive.

He was towering over her again and as he reached out and shook her hand, enclosing her small paw in his long, lean fingers, it took all of Kay's control not to snatch her hand away as she felt the contact of his flesh. Which was crazy, ridiculous, she told herself desperately, as were the ripples in her blood as the faint but delicious smell of him teased her nostrils for a second or two.

'Goodbye, Mrs Sherwood.' Mitchell Grey was fully aware that the small, slender girl in front of him had appeared to tell him plenty but in fact had said nothing— about herself, that was. With her mop of shoulder-length curls and Pollyanna freckles that stood out on her creamy skin like sprinkled spice, she was definitely not his type. No way. His women were elegant, exquisitely dressed and cosmopolitan, and more importantly they knew the score. A good time and plenty of fun and laughs on both sides while it lasted. And he always made sure it didn't last *too* long, he thought grimly, watching her until she disappeared from view into the waiting lift.

So what had made him want to know more about— he consulted the card in his hand—Kay Sherwood? he asked himself silently, vaguely irritated with himself.

A scrubbed and sweet-sixteen type if ever he saw one.
Although she wasn't sixteen, was she. And she was a
married woman—or had been married, someone who had
started a fledgling business in the present uneasy climate
and succeeded at it too.

His frown deepened. Most people who started up in
business on their own gained their first business experi-
ences in another job. Then they adapted a special skill or
special knowledge to a new idea, or branched out on their
own thinking they could do better than the company they
worked for. The young woman who had just walked out
of the office—Mitchell refused to dwell on the memory
of the rounded bottom under the leathers swaying pro-
vocatively as she'd disappeared—had plunged in without
all that, which showed she had plenty of guts and determination. So what was her story?

And then he mentally shrugged all thoughts of Kay
Sherwood away. He was already late for a business appointment in the heart of London and his chauffeur had
been waiting for fifteen minutes. What was he standing
here for? The hard, astute business brain kicked in and he
strode over to the lift, now utterly focused on the coming
meeting, which he knew would be a difficult one. As the
doors opened he slipped the business card in the top
pocket of his jacket, but not before a small separate section of his mind had filed away the name and telephone
number for future reference.

'So what was so bad about him asking you a few questions
about the business, Kay?' Kay's mother's brown eyes were
puzzled, understandably so, Kay had to admit. When she
actually repeated what Mitchell Grey had said word for
word it didn't convey anything of the man's arrogance or
the atmosphere that had been present between them.

'He was—well...just altogether irritating,' she finished lamely.

Leonora stared at her daughter for a moment more before saying diplomatically, 'Well, forget about him now, okay? It's doubtful if your paths will ever cross again and you've enough on your plate to concern yourself with as it is. You haven't forgotten it's the school's autumn fête this evening?'

'The twins wouldn't let me.' Kay smiled wryly and her mother smiled back.

'They're two live wires,' Leonora Brown admitted ruefully. 'But you were like that at their age, into everything and the whole world one gigantic adventure.'

Kay nodded, still smiling, but inwardly she was thinking, I was like that right up to the time I met Perry and then it was like I changed overnight. Why couldn't I see what he was doing to me?

She dropped her eyes from her mother's face, taking a sip of her coffee. They said love was blind, but in her case it had been a question of deaf, dumb *and* blind.

As her mother continued to chat on, the while chopping and slicing vegetables for the chicken casserole they were having for dinner, Kay gave every appearance of listening but her mind had taken a trip into the past.

She had gone out with Perry for a year before they had got married on her twenty-first birthday, the same month they had both finished at university, but within a couple of months of the wedding she had been forced to admit to herself she had made a terrible mistake. The cocoon of university life, and especially the last frantic year when she had worked as she'd never worked before, had masked so much that had been wrong in their relationship.

Perry had been young, good-looking and very charismatic, drawing people to him like moths to a flame with the power of his electric personality, but he had also been a cold-blooded, manipulative control freak—at least with her. She had been so crazy about him, and so busy—it having been her final year—that she hadn't even noticed that they'd done everything *his* way. But a few weeks into the marriage, due to a chance meeting with an old school-friend, she had been jolted free of the soporific bubble he'd carefully manufactured round her.

What had she been doing with herself? her old friend had asked in all innocence. Had she been ill? She looked terrible. Was she working too hard?

The conversation had been awkward on both sides and Kay hadn't prolonged the encounter, but when she had got home to the one-bedroomed flat in Belgravia she and Perry had been renting she had taken a long, hard look at herself in the bathroom mirror. Her hair had been strained into a tight knot at the back of her head—Perry hated it loose—and she'd been wearing no make-up—Perry disliked any artifice—but it hadn't been that so much as the drawn look to her mouth and the expression in her eyes that had brought her up short.

She looked dowdy and plain, she'd realised suddenly, glancing down at the dress she'd been wearing—one of many things Perry had insisted on buying her. She was killing herself trying to please Perry in every tiny thing rather than having to endure his cutting comments and icy silences when she said or did something he didn't agree with.

She'd stood there, in stunned shock, for some minutes. How long had this been going on? she'd asked herself numbly as reality had hit. They were happy, weren't they? She was so lucky to have him—wasn't she? He treated her so well, was so kind to her...

And the answer sounded in her head—everything was

wonderful when she was doing exactly as *he* wanted; he was the best husband in the world then. He told her how to dress, how to wear her hair; he was the one who decided when they went out and when they stayed in, even what programmes they watched on TV. Their friends were *his* friends; they ate the kind of food *he* liked and drank the wine he chose.

She had rubbed a shaky hand over her face, her mind racing. It hadn't been like that in the beginning, had it? Not for the first month or two. But then an insidious change had taken place and the most absurd thing, the preposterous, stupid and *unbelievable* thing, was that she hadn't seen it till now. She just hadn't realised it had been happening. Because he was such fun and so irresistible and mesmerising when he was being nice, it hadn't dawned on her that she was subconsciously subjugating her own persona all the time. It was as if she had turned into someone else, someone...alien. Even the fact that he had persuaded her not to look for a job immediately, but spend some time getting the flat round and creating a home for them now took on a new significance.

'I want to be able to picture you here when I'm away,' he had said beguilingly when she'd made noises about using her degree. 'Know you'll be here when I get home. We don't need your salary, darling, not at the moment, and, with me working for Dad, money will never be tight.'

She had stared at herself for some time that day. And then she'd run a hot bath, washed her hair and creamed herself all over with a frighteningly expensive body lotion that had been a Christmas present from her parents. After getting dressed in a pair of tight black jeans and little top she'd found pushed in the back of her wardrobe—remnants from pre-Perry days—she had carefully made up her face and teased her hair into soft waves about her face.

It had taken ages—her hair always wanted to go its own way and curl outrageously—but eventually she'd begun to recognise the girl in the mirror.

She had gone out and bought two steaks for dinner rather than labour over the chicken dhansak Perry had ordered, and she'd collected a paper detailing job vacancies at the same time.

When Perry had got home that evening he had found a dining table romantically set for two with candles and wine, a smiling, perfumed and groomed wife, and six envelopes containing job applications ready for posting. Even now she didn't like to think of the things he had said and how cruel he'd been, but it had been the beginning of the end.

By the time she had realised she was pregnant a little while later—she had been taking the pill but had been ill with a stomach upset at one point, not that that had stopped Perry from all but forcing himself on her one night—the discovery that Perry had begun an affair with one of the secretaries in his father's catering firm had finished the marriage completely. It had been a time of heartache and desperation and misery, but through it all she'd discovered she was stronger than she had suspected.

She had stayed on at the flat after she'd thrown Perry out, working right up to three weeks before the twins' birth and returning shortly after once she had found a good nursery. She had hated leaving them, but Perry's maintenance payments had not been forthcoming and as he had upped and left the area shortly after the birth she'd had little choice, other than moving back in with her parents. And somehow, and she couldn't have explained to a living soul why, that would have seemed like the final defeat, much as she loved her mother and father.

Then had come her father's massive heart attack, followed by the news his dabbling in the stock market had left his widow almost penniless. At the same time her married brother had lost his job just before his wife had been due to give birth to their second child.

Kay raised her head now, coming back to the present as she heard the front door slam. This meant their neighbour had dropped the twins off after school; several of them had got an efficient rota system established.

'Mummy!' As the kitchen door burst open and two little flame-haired figures catapulted into the room Kay prepared herself for the onslaught of small arms and legs with a feeling of deep thankfulness. Her girls were her life, her breath, her reason for living. They had brought her through the worst period of her life, her nurture of their tiny bodies in her womb meaning she hadn't been able to let herself sink into the abyss of despair she'd felt at the time of her marriage breakup, and their birth filling her with wonder and joy that these two tiny, perfect little babies were really hers. All hers.

'Mummy, I got a gold star today for sitting as still as a mouse during storytime.'

'And Miss Henson's put my picture on the wall. It's you, Mummy, and Grandma.'

'A picture's not as good as a gold star, is it, Mummy?'

'It is. It is as good. Better! Isn't it, Mummy?'

Both Georgia and Emily had clambered onto her lap, their arms wrapped round her neck as they struggled for prime position, all but choking her in the process.

She was saved by the ringing of the proverbial bell.

'It's for you.' Her mother had answered the telephone, which had begun to ring just as the twins had entered the room, and as Kay disentangled herself, kissing both small faces and telling them they were very clever girls, the older woman hissed quietly, 'It's him, Kay. That Mr Grey you told me about.'

'*What?*' Her mother had her hand over the mouthpiece, which was just as well considering how high-pitched Kay's voice had suddenly become.

Leonora now flapped her hand frantically as she pressed the receiver against her chest, mouthing, 'Quiet, he'll hear you.'

Kay looked down at the telephone as though it would scald her, making no effort to take it as she whispered back, 'How do you know it's him?'

'He said, of course, unless you know more than one Mitchell Grey?'

How on earth had he got this number? The card had given the office number but that was all. Kay took the phone, holding it gingerly as she said, 'Hallo? This is Kay Sherwood.'

'Good evening, Mrs Sherwood.' The deep voice held the texture of seductively soft velvet over finely honed steel. 'I hope you don't mind my calling you at home; I did try the number you gave me but a Mr Brown—your brother, I understand?—told me I was more likely to catch you at home at this time of the day.'

Cheers, thanks, Peter. Kay tried to inject a note of enthusiasm into her voice when she said, 'Not at all, Mr Grey. How can I help you?'

There was the briefest of pauses before the compelling voice spoke again. 'I wondered if you are free tomorrow evening?'

It would be true to say Kay had never been so surprised in her life. She knew her mouth had dropped open, and something in her face even stopped the squabbling of the twins because they, like her mother, were now staring at her curiously.

Kay's brain was racing, her thoughts tumbling over each other. He couldn't mean he was suggesting a date? He couldn't, could he? No, he must mean some sort of job. An evening delivery maybe? That must be it.

And then she was disabused of this idea when he added, 'I've tickets for the theatre, and I thought perhaps a spot of dinner first?'

Say something, Kay told herself. Anything. Except yes. She moistened her lips. 'I'm sorry, Mr Grey, but I'm busy tomorrow night,' she lied politely.

'Next week some time?'

She stared frantically at the three very interested faces at the kitchen table, and when no help was forthcoming said carefully, 'I'm sorry but this is really a very busy time for us at the moment and it's all hands to the plough.'

'You don't take time out to eat?' he asked smoothly, continuing before she had a chance to reply, 'How about lunch instead, then? And before you tell me how sorry you are again, perhaps I ought to mention that I was hoping to discuss a business proposition I had in mind.'

So it hadn't been a date! Kay was so relieved she spoke without thinking, not realising how her voice had changed. 'A business proposition? Oh, of course, Mr Grey,' she said eagerly. 'Shall we say Monday?'

'Let's.' It was dry in the extreme. 'I'll call at your office at one o'clock. Goodbye, Mrs Sherwood.'

And he had put down the phone before it dawned on her that one didn't normally suggest theatre and dinner to discuss a business proposal.

CHAPTER TWO

IF KAY picked up the telephone once on Monday morning to cancel her lunch with Mitchell Grey, she picked it up a hundred times. She'd thought of little else during the weekend, going over their conversation in her mind until her brain was buzzing and her nerves were frazzled.

One moment she was telling herself that it was the height of arrogance to think that a man like him—clearly very wealthy, successful and drop-dead gorgeous—would ask her for a date, and that the proposed meeting must—*must*—be a business one. Then the memory of his voice when he had suggested the theatre and dinner would reverberate in her head, firing the panic button.

She had telephoned Peter as soon as she had put down the phone from Mitchell Grey on Friday afternoon, but her brother hadn't been particularly helpful.

'Why did I give him your home number?' Peter said breezily when she challenged him. 'Well, why not? It's not a secret, is it? You're not ex-directory or anything like that.'

Kay bit down on her lip and prayed for patience. She loved Peter dearly, and his wife and two boys meant a great deal to her, but just at that moment in time she could have hit him hard without a shred of remorse.

After a few more minutes of questioning, Peter grew impatient. 'What do you mean, how did he sound?' he asked her irritably. 'What sort of dumb question is that? I *told* you—he phoned up and wanted to speak to you, said he'd talked to you earlier in the day and there was something more he wanted to discuss. When I said you weren't around he asked if you'd got a number where he could contact you, and so I said yes. Not the deepest or most meaningful conversation in the world admittedly, but there it is.'

Kay mentally cancelled the new sound system she'd been planning to buy him for Christmas and substituted a pair of socks instead. 'I don't want to see him,' she said tightly.

'Don't, then.' Peter spoke with true brotherly compassion.

'It's not as easy as that. What if he *does* want to discuss something that would do the firm some good? What then?'

'Kay, correct me if I'm wrong but we're talking lunch here, aren't we? The guy isn't suggesting you go up and see his etchings or nip off to Bournemouth for a dirty weekend. What's your problem?'

She slammed the phone down then, telling the twins their uncle was the most irritating man in the world before they all got ready to leave for the autumn fête whereby her mind was taken off Mitchell Grey for a little while.

Peter's last words came back to her now as she glanced nervously at her wrist-watch. Ten minutes and counting. She shut her eyes tightly for a second before she opened them again, speaking out loud into the small office they rented on the ground floor of a converted house. 'So, what *is* your problem?'

She didn't know, she admitted miserably, which wasn't like her. She was a practical person at heart, not given to flights of fancy or goose-pimply feelings, but there was something about Mitchell Grey...

It didn't help that both Peter and Tom were out on deliveries either, which meant she was waiting all alone

without any conversation to take her mind off the forthcoming encounter. Peter might be the most exasperating
soul on earth at times, and Tom could be nearly as bad,
but at least there was never a dull moment when the two
of them were around. Of course she could have wandered
in to either the watch repairer's or the accountant's—the
two other offices on the ground floor of the premises—
and passed the time of day for a while, but with no one
else to man the phone it would have been an indulgence.

She glanced down at her lightly structured jacket and
short skirt in shot blue silk, which had cost her an arm
and a leg in the summer, and which had been bought for
the wedding of her cousin, and again blessed the fact that
the October day was mild and sunny. She hadn't spent
much on decent clothes lately—the twins always seemed
to outgrow their shoes before she could blink and there
always were a hundred and one things to buy before she
indulged herself—but then she didn't really need anything. Her leathers were her working clothes, and the nearest she ever got to going out was taking the twins to the
park or swimming at the local pool.

Had she scrubbed up sufficiently well to hold her own
on a lunch appointment with Mitchell Grey? For the ump-
teenth time since she'd arrived at the office that morning
she opened the bottom drawer of her desk and fished out
the small hand mirror she kept there.

Wide brown eyes set under brows that were fine and
straight stared back anxiously, a couple of coats of mas-
cara the only make-up she was wearing. She patted one
or two errant curls back into the high loose pony-tail on
top of her head, the style deceptively casual considering
it had taken an hour to complete first thing that morning.

'You have beautiful hair.'

Her head shot up at the same time as she hastily threw

the mirror back into the drawer, slamming it shut and breaking a nail in the process.

Mitchell Grey was standing just inside the open office door, and in the same moment that Kay registered the hard, handsome face, full of sharply defined angles and planes made all the more threatening by the jet-black hair, she mentally cursed the fact that, after her being on watch the whole morning, he had to sneak up on her at the very moment she was at a disadvantage.

Her voice reflected some of what she was feeling when she said, 'Mr Grey. I didn't hear you come in.'

He raised his eyebrows, his voice lazy and faintly amused. 'I apologise.'

'No, I didn't mean—' She stopped abruptly. She *had* meant, actually, she told herself ungrammatically, and she was blowed if she was going to say otherwise, business proposition or no business proposition. She compressed her soft mouth, and then saw his lips twitch with a dart of fury. He thought this was funny, did he? He thought *she* was funny?

She rose to her feet as gracefully as her old saggy chair would allow, tweaking her skirt into place when she saw the silver eyes rest briefly on the inordinate amount of leg the action had revealed. 'You found us all right, then?' She moved across to him with her hand outstretched, determined to seize hold of the situation.

He nodded, his voice now holding the sort of gentleness that suggested he was humouring her when he said, 'My chauffeur was born and bred in these parts; I don't think there's an alley or back way he isn't familiar with.'

His chauffeur. Oh, wow. But of course a man like Mitchell Grey would have a chauffeur, she told herself helplessly. He probably hadn't meant it that way but it was a subtle reminder that he was the one holding all the aces and that she couldn't afford to be touchy around him—not until she knew whether it was going to cost them hard cash, at least.

'You said something about a business proposition?' she asked him now as their hands connected.

'Let's get on our way first.'

He didn't have to ask twice. The feel of his warm, hard flesh had unnerved her every bit as much as it had before, and more so considering they were alone here. Besides which, she hadn't really appreciated just how tatty their premises were until he had walked in—designer perfection personified, she thought nastily, wishing she could honestly tell herself there were something of the dandy about him but knowing it wouldn't be true. He was all male. Intimidatingly so.

She found herself fumbling with the key as she locked the door to the office, vitally aware of the tall figure waiting for her by the front door of the building, and once they emerged into the busy street and he took her elbow it was all she could do not to pull away. 'The car's over here.' He guided her across the pavement full of lunchtime shoppers towards a long, sleek Bentley parked on double yellow lines, a uniformed chauffeur sitting impassively in the front seat.

Once in the leather-clad interior Kay had a brief tussle with her skirt before sitting as primly as it would allow. Why hadn't she noticed how short it was at Caroline's wedding? she asked herself as a mortifyingly large expanse of nylon-clad flesh made itself known. Probably because Mitchell Grey wasn't at the nuptials was the answer to that, she admitted irritably.

'Relax, Kay.'

The shock of hearing her name spoken by the richly dark voice brought her head swinging round to meet his gaze, and she saw the silver-blue eyes were narrowed thoughtfully on her face.

'I beg your pardon?' She tried for icy hauteur but the effect was ruined by her breathlessness. He was close, very close in the confines of the car, and like once before the subtle sexy aftershave he wore had her pulse rate flying.

'You're tense, keyed up,' he said soothingly, 'and there is no need to be, really. Look, would it help if I came clean and admitted right now that there is no business proposition? That this is intended to be just a nice meal in comfortable surroundings where we can chat and get to know each other a little?'

Would it help? Would it—? 'Stop the car!'

'I'm sorry?'

Even if it had been possible for so ruthless and attractive a man to look innocent, his mild response to her yelp of outrage wouldn't have deceived her. She glared at him, her face flushed and her mouth set, and it was incredibly galling to see he wasn't in the least ashamed of himself.

'I said, stop the car,' Kay ground out through clenched teeth.

'All in good time.' And he had the effrontery to try a smile that she supposed he imagined made him irresistible. 'I want to explain first. You had clearly made up your mind that you didn't want to see me again—'

'How right you are,' she snarled softly.

'And so all this deception is entirely your fault,' he continued silkily.

'*My* fault?'

'Of course.' He had settled back in the seat as he'd spoken and he was so obviously enjoying her discomfiture that Kay would have slapped him if she'd dared. But she didn't. Much as she hated to admit it to herself.

'Now look, Mr Grey, I don't know what sort of game you think you are playing but you've picked the wrong girl,' she said with acid sharpness. 'I don't like the caveman approach, if that's what you're thinking, and frankly I find your attitude offensive. I want out of this car and right now.' She fumbled with the handle but wasn't surprised to find the door was locked.

'Aren't you overreacting a little?' he asked mildly. 'All I want to do is to take you to lunch.'

This couldn't be happening. She couldn't really be locked in a car with a virtual stranger being taken to goodness knew where. She took the last thought a step further when she said, 'My mother knows I have a luncheon engagement with you today, Mr Grey, as well as my brother.'

'I should hope so. It would be very unwise not to inform at least one person of your whereabouts in this day and age in which we live,' he said smoothly.

The dark head had turned to look out of the window a few moments before but now he turned back to face her, one dark eyebrow quirked mockingly as he added, 'We're here. Now try to act your age and pretend you are a cool and contained businesswoman being brought out to lunch by a male colleague, okay? That will save us both any embarrassment.'

Embarrassment? She couldn't imagine Mitchell Grey ever suffering that emotion in the whole of his life. There was arrogance, and then there was this man, and she didn't even have a word to describe him. Not one she could repeat in civilised company, anyway. If anyone needed taking down a peg or two it was him.

She glanced out of the window of the car as it drew to a stop outside a restaurant she had heard about but never entered—mainly because the cost of a meal there would necessitate taking out a second mortgage—and it was in that moment the idea occurred to her. She glanced at the big dark figure next to her and found his gaze was on her face, a disturbing gleam at the back of his eyes. What was he thinking? What did he expect her to do right at this moment? She rather suspected he was prepared for the fact that she might turn tail and march off, and she really wouldn't put it past him to manhandle her into the building, awkward though it would be for both of them.

He was a control freak if ever she'd met one—and she had, first hand, she thought tightly as Perry's face flashed across the screen of her mind for a second. But she wasn't going to put up with this, not for a moment. Her starry-eyed devotion to Perry had nearly ruined her life and the days had long since gone when she would allow a man to dictate to her.

It had been an uphill struggle for months when, after her father had died and her mother had needed her, she had come back to Romford, leaving her London flat and taking out a mortgage on the tiny house they now all lived in. Her salary had not allowed her to take on more than a small, two-bedroomed place, and even then Ivy Cottage had been dilapidated and in need of renovation. But the 1920's former ale house had had an endearing air about it, the two bedrooms overlooking what once had been a pretty garden filled with topiary, flower borders, a rockery and even an original brick well, but on their first visit to view had resembled a miniature jungle.

Her father's bad investments had meant her mother had brought nothing to the kitty, but gradually, with lots of help from Peter and his friends, they had repaired and painted and made good, transforming shabby into chic. Now the panelled front door of Ivy Cottage opened into a beamed sitting room with an open fireplace, which was cosy and charming, the kitchen-diner adequate for their needs, although Kay had to admit there wasn't room to swing a cat when Peter and his family came round for a meal. But with the twins in one bedroom and Kay and her mother sharing the other, they were happy, and the garden had proved to be a little oasis all year round. Most of all, though, the move back to Romford had saved her mother from slipping into the nervous breakdown the doctor had said was imminent. Leonora had had to take on the care of the twins during the day while Kay worked— nursery fees now being out of the question—and being wanted and useful again, as well as having her daughter and grandchildren with her permanently, had been the stimulant the older woman had needed.

It had been a fight to survive for a while after Perry had gone, but she had not only survived but managed to provide a secure home for the girls and her mother as well as establishing what was now a thriving little business, Kay thought as she climbed out of the car, ignoring Mitchell Grey's outstretched hand. There was no way she was being walked over by this arrogant brute of a man, and he was going to learn that the hard way very soon. She was self-governing now, independent.

She walked ahead of him into the restaurant, a strange prickly sensation running up and down her spine as they paused just within the doors and he took her elbow, speaking to the head waiter who had flown to their side. 'Ah, Angelo. You have my table ready?'

'Of course, Mr Grey.'

The man didn't actually bow them to the small discreet table set at an angle where they could see but not be on view, but the obsequiousness was enough to set Kay's teeth further on edge. If people were like this with Mitchell Grey no wonder the man's ego was inflated to jumbo size!

'Would you like a cocktail while you look at the menu?' The wine waiter had appeared at their side the moment they'd been seated. 'I can recommend the Smouldering Liaison,' Mitchell Grey said, blandly enough but Kay had noticed the lingering amusement curling his mouth.

'Cocktails in the lunch hour?' She raised what she hoped were coldly disapproving eyebrows.

'I'm not driving.' He settled back in his seat, pulling his tie loose and undoing the first couple of buttons of his shirt as he spoke. 'Are you?'

Kay cleared her dry throat. His powerful masculinity was all the more flagrant for its casual unconsciousness and she didn't like the way her body had reacted to what was a perfectly normal action on his part. 'No,' she admitted coolly. Peter and Tom were handling the driving for today, and although Peter had picked her up in one of the vans that morning she had planned to take a taxi for the short ride home, knowing her brother would be late back. 'But I like to be alert in the afternoon.'

'I'm sure you do.'

Four small words, but he managed to make them sound insulting, Kay thought angrily. She bit back on the hot words burning her tongue, glancing at the cocktail menu again. Perhaps she *would* have a drink at that, she decided. She needed a spot of Dutch courage if she was going to carry out her idea to put Mitchell Grey in his place.

''I'll have a Sweet Revenge, please,' she said primly, choosing the cocktail purely for its name rather than the mix of coconut rum, gin, tequila and banana essence it contained.

He whistled slowly through his teeth. 'Are you sure? It has a kick like a mule.'

'Revenge always has.' She smiled sweetly. She wanted him to remember what she'd chosen for a long, long time.

He shrugged broad shoulders. 'A Sweet Revenge for the lady,' he said lazily to the waiter, 'and I'll have a Wolf in Sheep's Clothing.'

Except in this case it was definitely a wolf in wolf's clothing, Kay thought, staring at the hard, rugged profile in the moment before he turned his head and looked at her again. And she certainly wasn't Little Red Riding Hood.

'How long are you going to be annoyed with me?' he asked her softly after a couple of seconds had ticked by.

She forced herself not to lower her gaze although the ice-blue eyes with their silver hue were piercing. 'You think I should be grateful you tricked me into having lunch with you?'

'Not exactly.' His eyes glinted at her and she knew he wasn't taking any of this seriously. It was more galling than words could express. 'But surely there are worse crimes than taking a beautiful woman out to eat?'

'You insinuated you had work for my firm.' If he thought he could sweet talk her he had another think coming. Beautiful woman indeed! Kay refused to acknowledge her accelerating pulse.

'But you'd already told me you had more work than you knew what to do with so I didn't think you'd mind too much.' He smiled. Kay did not. 'Added to which I had tried the honest approach first only to be shot down in flames. You left me with no other option,' he cajoled silkily.

This was a ridiculous conversation. She stared coldly at him, willing her fluttering heart to behave. His smoky warm voice and the sexy curve to his mouth were part of a blatant seduction programme, that was as clear as the nose on his face. Probably he'd tried this approach before and it had worked like a dream; she didn't think he got turned down too often. In fact it was very probable he had never got turned down before. It just showed you were never too old for a new experience, she told herself with secret relish.

The waiter arrived with their cocktails before she had a chance to say anything, the head waiter popping up like a genie out of a bottle a moment later with two elaborate and heavily embossed menus. 'The lobster and scallops with caviare garnish is highly recommended today, Mr Grey,' he murmured smoothly. 'Or perhaps the black leg chicken with wild mushrooms and asparagus? I'll leave you to contemplate for a few moments.'

'Thank you, Angelo. And could we have a bottle of that rather pleasant Moët et Chandon I had last time, the rosé? You do like rosé champagne?' he added, turning to Kay as he spoke the last words.

'I drink little else,' she replied with a brittle smile. If he thought he could buy her with a bottle of good champagne he was even more arrogant than she'd supposed.

The head waiter bustled off, after a somewhat nervous glance in Kay's direction, and she hastily took a sip of her creamy yellow cocktail. It was okay until it hit the back of her throat, and then the delicious taste was superseded by eye-watering heat. He hadn't exaggerated the kick of the mule bit, Kay was forced to acknowledge, and then—aware of a quietly amused gaze trained on her face—she forced herself to take another sip. It wasn't so bad now she was prepared for it, and she didn't glance directly across the table until the moisture in her eyes had subsided and she was fully in control of herself.

'Delicious,' she said serenely.

'I'm glad you like it,' he returned gravely.

Sarcastic swine. Kay made a great play of studying the menu. She felt hot and flustered and she was determined not to let it show. She was going to be dignified and icy to the end or die in the attempt.

The head waiter did his rabbit-out-of-a-hat trick in the next instant, seemingly materialising out of thin air and taking their order with profuse delight. As he glided away Kay glanced round the softly lighted, elegant surroundings, the low hum of gentle conversation and the general air of affluence suiting the bon viveur diners perfectly.

It would be better if she ate her first course before putting her plan into action; it would lull him into a false sense of security and have more effect in the long run. So... Conversation. She had to at least appear to have accepted the status quo.

'Mr Grey—'

'Mitchell, please,' he reproved her gently.

Kay nodded stiffly. 'Mitchell,' she continued evenly, 'I really don't see why it was so important I accepted a dinner invitation with you. I should imagine there are any number of women who would be only too pleased to accompany you.'

He settled himself further into his chair, finishing his cocktail and placing the empty glass on the table before he said, 'Possibly.' And if he were truthful he would have added that he didn't understand fully why he had pursued what was obviously a non-starter either. He prided himself on being a very rational and judicious man; irrationalism was not an option. So what was it about this slender woman with her mop of hair and freckles that had got under his skin? Much as he hated to admit it, he hadn't been able to get her out of his mind for more than a few minutes at a time since he'd set eyes on her.

Kay stared at him. Possibly—was that all he was going to say on the matter? He met her gaze, his eyes crystal-sharp and unblinking, his sensual mouth curved cynically.

'But you didn't feel inclined to take advantage of their services?' she asked with deliberate innuendo.

He smiled lazily. 'Are you casting aspersions on my ability to acquire a woman, Kay? I can assure you I have never needed to pay for one.'

'I didn't think for a minute you had.' And she hadn't— it had just been rather a cheap jibe to annoy him, she admitted silently, not liking herself. She wouldn't have dreamt of behaving like this normally; it was all his fault!

'Good.' He looked at her quietly for a moment. 'Tell me a little about yourself.'

'I thought I already had.' She forced a quick smile. 'It's your turn, surely? How would your CV read?'

'Well, let's see.' The wine waiter appeared with the champagne in an ice bucket. Mitchell waited until all the formalities of tasting and such were out of the way and they were alone again before he continued, 'Name, Mitchell Charles Grey. Age, thirty-five. Marital status, single, Mother, Irish, Father, English, both died in a car crash when I was fifteen. I started my own company at the age of twenty by investing all my inheritance in it along with a whopping great bank loan, and by the age of thirty had branched out to include premises in Southampton, Portsmouth and Plymouth. Anything else you'd like to know?'

Masses, and she didn't like that, Kay acknowledged, a sudden tightness in her chest. She didn't want to be interested in this man, not in any way. 'You're very successful,' she prevaricated carefully.

He nodded. False modesty was obviously not one of his failings.

'And happy?' she added evenly.

'Happy?' He didn't answer immediately, his eyes narrowing. 'Happiness is such a fragile emotion, don't you think? And not one I believe in, to be honest.'

'No?' She couldn't help it, she had to know more. 'So what *do* you believe in?'

'Hard work, determination, wealth, success. The first two giving rise to the latter when combined with that magical element called luck.'

'Right.' She finished her cocktail and hoped the waiter would bring the watercress soufflé and wholemead bread she'd ordered for her starter very soon. She was feeling distinctly light-headed. She looked at her glass of sparkling champagne and knew she didn't dare try even a sip until she'd eaten something. 'So you're a self-made man who enjoys his autonomy. Would that be a fair summing up?' she asked calmly.

'I dare say.' His brow crinkled into a quizzical ruffle. 'How about you? Are you a self-made woman who enjoys *her* autonomy?'

Self-made woman was on the grand side for her little tuppenny enterprise compared with Grey Cargo International, but Kay didn't feel inclined to point that out right now. She nodded. 'Yes.'

'And is there a current boyfriend lurking in the background somewhere?' he asked casually.

That would be the day. She'd had one or two dates in the last three years but only when she'd made it absolutely clear it was on a friends-only basis. Apart from the fact that she had no intention of introducing the odd 'uncle' to the twins, she simply didn't want to ever get heavily involved with a man again, or at least not for the foreseeable future. Maybe when the twins were grown up and off her hands she might consider a relationship if the right man came along, but he would have to understand that the whole marriage thing, even a for-ever type commitment, was out of the question. She had gone there and done that, she had the mental and emotional scars to prove it. She would never give anyone power over her like that again.

Kay took a deep breath. 'A boyfriend?' she said evenly. 'No. I haven't got the time or the inclination for romantic attachments of any kind.'

He shifted in his chair, leaning towards her as he said, 'That's a little harsh, isn't it? Was your marriage really that bad?'

She had absolutely no intention of discussing her marriage or anything else of a personal nature with this man. She looked into the hard, handsome face, folding her hands in her lap to emphasise she was perfectly relaxed and in control. 'It's over,' she said coolly, 'and I never look back or discuss the past.'

'In other words I can mind my own business?' He folded his arms over his chest, contemplating her with the penetrating, astute gaze she found so disturbing. 'What about a family in the future, children? Aren't you a bit young to close the door on that?'

She didn't answer this directly. What she did say was, 'What about you? Is that what you want—hearth, home and family?' her tone disbelieving.

He gave her a hard look before a grudging smile touched the carved lips. *'Touché,'* he murmured softly. 'No, as you've so rightly discerned, that is not what I want. I don't see myself as a family man. Children deserve absolute commitment, both from parents to the child and from parent to parent, and the possibility of wanting to stay faithful to the same woman for the rest of one's life seems ludicrous to me. And if one party does stray it can make family life hell on earth.'

His face had remained the same as he'd spoken but there had been something, just the faintest note in his voice, that made Kay say, 'Is that what happened to you as a child?' before she could stop herself.

For a moment she thought he wasn't going to answer her, and then he said, his voice very even, 'This is getting a little deep for a lunchtime chat, isn't it?' There followed the briefest of pauses before he added, 'Yes, that is what happened to me,' and, looking beyond her, 'Ah, here comes the food. I trust you will find it enjoyable. I find the chef here one of the best I've come across.'

Kay felt thoroughly put in her place. Why, oh, why had she asked him that? She hadn't meant to. Here was she determined not to reveal a thing about herself and she had gone and asked him something so personal that even a close friend would have hesitated to intrude. She began to eat the soufflé without tasting it, her cheeks burning.

'It's all right, Kay.'

The quiet voice brought her eyes up from the soufflé dish and she found he was looking at her, unsmiling but with a curious expression on his face. With anyone else but Mitchell Grey she would have thought it was gentleness.

'If I hadn't wanted to answer I wouldn't have done. Okay?'

He'd known she felt bad. She could feel her cheeks glowing still more as she nodded before saying, 'I had no right to ask such a personal question; we're strangers, after all.'

'I would like to think that isn't quite true.'

She lowered her gaze and began to eat again, her taste

buds telling her the soufflé was a dream and her mind screaming at her that she had to get out of here.

Something had changed and shifted in the last few minutes, something intangible but very real and infinitely dangerous. And she didn't mind admitting she didn't know how to handle it—or perhaps she should say she didn't know how to handle Mitchell Grey. Whatever, it was time to put her original idea into action.

She had finished the soufflé and now she put the last portion of delicious home-made bread into her mouth, swallowing it quickly before she said, 'Excuse me a moment; I need to powder my nose,' and she reached for her handbag.

'Sure.' As she rose to her feet he stood too and Kay acknowledged that the old-fashioned courtesy surprised her. 'The cloakrooms are over the far side of the room,' he said quietly.

'Thank you.' She gave him a brief smile and then forced herself not to hurry as she walked in the direction he had indicated. Just before she went through the door to the ladies' cloakroom she glanced back towards their table. He was seated again, his eyes on her as he drank his champagne. There was a brooding quality to his stance and for a second Kay found it difficult to look away. Then she opened the door to the cloakroom and stepped into the scented interior.

For a moment after the door had closed behind her she stood quite still, her heart thumping so hard it was painful. There was no one else with her, and she glanced round the ultra-deluxe room with its beautifully tiled white and gold walls and granite surfaces in which three washbasins were set, before making her way to the window.

Thank goodness the cloakroom wasn't an inner room, but did the windows open, and, if so, onto what? The modern frame had one large fixed pane of glass with two top-hung smaller windows either side of it, all with heavily opaque privacy glass.

Kay glanced at the locks on the smaller windows; there was no key that she could see. Please open, she prayed, please, *please* open. Her heart in her mouth, she tried the one nearest to her and felt a flood of relief as it swung outwards. It opened onto what appeared to be a small yard containing several large plastic dustbins in one corner and various other containers dotted about the limited space.

Directly below the window the area was clear, but it looked to be something like a six- or seven-foot drop to the ground. That wouldn't have mattered if she had been in jeans or trousers, but her short, slimline skirt didn't lend itself easily to mountaineering.

So, what were the options? Kay stepped back from the open window and turned to face the room as she ran things over in her mind. Did she let Mitchell Grey get away with tricking her here and all but forcing her to eat with him? No, not *all* but forcing her, she corrected herself in the next moment. He *had* forced her. She had decided to teach him a lesson in the car and she still intended to go through with it...didn't she? The moment of doubt was enough to put steel in her backbone. He had been trying to charm her out there but he had picked the wrong girl and she wasn't fooled for a minute. She wouldn't *let* herself be fooled. Not ever again. Perry had had the sweet talk and beguilement down to a fine art and could be Mr Irresistible himself—when he was getting his own way.

Kay bent down, slipping off her high-heeled shoes and holding them in one hand as she mentally prepared herself. She was going to look pretty silly if anyone came into the cloakroom in the next few minutes but that couldn't be helped. Better that than letting Mitchell Grey think he could bully her into submission!

There was a small upholstered chair in one corner of the cloakroom and now she lifted it over to below the window, taking a long deep breath before stepping up on it. She dropped her shoes out of the window onto the ground below, hearing them thud with a dart of fatalism. She was committed to the escape now; she could hardly pad back out there with bare feet.

She moved her shoulder bag so it was hanging on her back and clambered from the chair onto the window sill, her skirt riding almost up to her waist. She had never felt so silly in all her life. What *must* she look like from the rear? she asked herself with a little giggle of near hysteria. So much for the cool, collected businesswoman image.

The aperture was just about big enough for her to squeeze through although once or twice in all her wriggling and squirming she thought she was stuck. Only the thought of just how much Mitchell Grey would relish such a predicament kept her from giving up.

She had twisted round on the sill before worming her way out of the window backwards, which was just as well, because suddenly she emerged like a cork out of a bottle onto the ground below, grazing her knees on the wall on her way down. The air turned a delicate shade of blue as she picked herself up, examining her torn tights and bloody knees. Great. Just great.

Picking up her bag from where it had fallen in the rapid descent, she opened it, extracting a tissue and dabbing at her knees. Ow... She'd forgotten the pain of grazed knees but now she was transported back into childhood again. She must remember to give the twins due sympathy next time one of them fell off their bicycles, a fairly regular occurrence.

After dusting herself down and bundling as much of her hair as she could back into the pony-tail, Kay pulled on her shoes and limped off to the gate set in the high brick wall that surrounded the yard. It was bolted in two places but the bolts slid easily beneath her fingers; obviously the gate was in regular use. She stepped out from the yard into the side street, glancing about her rather like a fugitive from the law who expected a Bonnie and Clyde ambush any moment. Apart from a fat tabby cat busily eating something disgusting from an overturned dustbin some yards away, all was quiet, but the main street was just a little way along the pavement.

As she emerged into the busier road she saw the welcome sight of a taxi approaching and all but threw herself into its path, but it wasn't until she had given her home address and the vehicle was on its way again that it dawned on her she had actually *done* it. She had left Mitchell Grey sitting waiting for her in that swish restaurant with his grand bottle of champagne slowly losing its bubbles. It wouldn't be long before their main course would be brought to the table; how long would he continue to wait after that before he asked for someone, a waitress maybe, to find her? He was going to look such a fool...

She stared out of the window at the shops and buildings flashing by, and wondered why there was none of the pleasure she had anticipated in her victory, but only a feeling of consuming flatness.

CHAPTER THREE

'GOOD grief, child, whatever will you do next?'

Her mother had spoken as if she were a little girl again, and to be truthful that was exactly how Kay felt as she stood in the kitchen, clutching her torn tights and with her bruised and bloody knees on show. She had just given Leonora the bare outline of what had occurred, and the older woman had sat down with a sudden plump before she'd spoken.

'He deserved it.' There was more than a touch of defensiveness in Kay's voice.

'I'm not saying he didn't, although there are worse crimes than abducting someone to the sort of restaurant he took you to.' Leonora shook her head slowly, her still lovely face unable to hide her amazement.

'That's what he said.' Kay surveyed her mother with guarded eyes. 'But I don't appreciate being lied to or forced into accompanying someone somewhere when I'd made it clear I wanted to leave.'

'No, I can understand that.' Leonora rose from the stool. 'I'll make us both a coffee, shall I, while you have a shower and change? Are you going back to the office today?'

'No. Peter and Tom are both out and the answer machine can deal with any calls. People will have to try elsewhere if it's urgent. I thought I might meet the girls out of school. They'd like that.'

'They'd love it,' Leonora agreed softly. She was well aware of the real reason her daughter was doing the unheard of and taking an afternoon off, but thought it advisable not to refer to it. If Mitchell Grey should go to the office she wouldn't like Kay to be there alone, the sort of rage he would probably be in. No...a man like that—proud, ruthless—would almost certainly just cut his losses, Leonora assured herself hopefully as she watched her daughter leave the room.

Once upstairs in the minute but pretty lemon and blue bathroom, which was just big enough to hold a shower, toilet and hand basin, Kay undressed quickly. She was feeling a bit shaky, she admitted reluctantly, but it was just reaction, added to which she'd had that enormous cocktail and eaten very little. She wasn't in the least bothered about how Mitchell Grey would view her unceremonious departure from the restaurant and his life—she *wasn't*.

Just let him try any intimidation of any kind or turn nasty and she would— Well, she didn't know what she'd do, she confessed weakly, stepping under the warm water and letting the silky flow caress her. But she was not going to be bullied—that much was for sure.

After a minute or two she stirred herself to begin washing her hair, massaging her scalp with unnecessary vigour as though she could wash the thoughts tumbling about her head away with the perfumed suds. Once dry again, she daubed a liberal amount of antiseptic cream on her knees—gritting her teeth when it stung like sulphuric acid—before covering the raw patches with two enormous plasters.

After pulling on a pair of jeans and a big fluffy cream jumper, she conditioned and dried her hair but couldn't be bothered to engage in the normal fight to tame it. She let it fall about her face and shoulders in a mass of riotous red-brown silky curls and waves, aware it made her look about sixteen but uncaring. Her wild mop was the least of her problems.

It wasn't until she was ready to go downstairs just after her mother had called her to say the coffee was ready that Kay admitted to herself she'd behaved incredibly badly.

She paused on the small landing, shutting her eyes for a moment. Not that he'd acted any better, she told herself in the next moment—lying to her and forcing her to enter the restaurant—but it wasn't like her to be unkind. Oh, hell... She groaned softly, sitting down on the top stair and kneading the back of her neck, which was as taut as piano wire. But it was done now and he *had* asked for it—or some sort of retaliation at least. Sweet Revenge... She was sure it was that lethal cocktail that had given her the mother and father of a headache.

Kay walked the half-mile or so to the twins' school. The mild sunny day was mellowing into the sort of late October evening when woodsmoke and falling leaves provided a touch of pure English magic. It was usually at times like this that she reflected how lucky she was. She had her precious girls, a lovely home and the sort of job that made the nine-to-five slog interesting and absorbing. Tonight, however, was different.

She was unsettled, she admitted irritably. All at odds with herself. And Mitchell Grey was to blame. Not only had he tried to kidnap her but he now had her almost apologising for resisting it! She must be mad. She wasn't going to give him or the day's events another thought.

'If you can't take the heat stay out of the kitchen,' she muttered to herself aggressively as she reached the school gates. 'And that's for you, Mitchell Grey.'

After seeing the neighbour whose turn it had been to take the twins home, Kay waited for the two little girls to come out into the playground. She wasn't disappointed by their reaction when they caught sight of her and—as always at times like this—she felt the stab of guilt that she couldn't meet them more often. But—and it was a big but—they still needed every penny the company could bring in to pay a living wage to herself, Peter and Tom. They all had families to support, and, although the company had proved itself to be a growing and successful one, the next step—that of taking on more employees and expanding—was a gamble. They'd all seen firms that had grown too quickly, and enlarged into disaster and liquidation, and with the girls and her mother depending on her she couldn't take any chances.

'Hard work, determination, wealth, success. The first two giving rise to the latter when combined with that magical element called luck.' Mitchell Grey's words rang in Kay's ears as she and the twins made their way home through the dusky air. Well, unlike Mr Grey who only answered to himself if things went wrong, she had people depending on her, Kay told herself crabbily. She couldn't afford the sort of Russian roulette speculation that could take a relative nobody to millionaire status in business. Of course someone like him, a self-confessed autonomist who had no time for long-term personal relationships, would have no such qualms.

'We're home!' As she opened the front door Kay called to her mother in the kitchen before standing aside for Georgia and Emily to precede her. They raced across the sitting room, flinging open the door into the kitchen.

As Kay closed the door behind her she became aware of two things in the same instant. The girls had skidded to an abrupt halt in the doorway and her mother was saying something, her words high and rushed, which indicated she was nervous. And then she heard the deep, smoky male voice, and she knew...

By the time she reached the doorway she had herself under control again, only the whiteness of her skin betraying that she was scared to death. Mitchell Grey was sitting at the table with her mother, a cup of coffee and an enormous wedge of Leonora's carrot cake in front of him.

Kay stared at him, knowing she had to say something but utterly bereft of words to meet the occasion. He stared back silently with unfathomable eyes.

'Kay, darling, there you are.' Leonora rose hastily from the table, all fluster, and moved round the long breakfast bar that divided the dining area from the kitchen. 'Mitchell called by to have a word. I'll take the girls into the sitting room, shall I?'

'Not on my account, please, Leonora.' He smiled at her as he spoke before glancing at the two little girls who were shyly clutching Kay's legs. 'Your grandmother has told me about you two. Now, which is which?'

Mitchell and Leonora? She had only been gone for just under an hour and in that time her mother and Mitchell Grey had become best buddies?

'I'm Georgia and she's Emily.' Georgia, always the least shy spoke up as she looked curiously at the big dark man dominating the tiny dining area. 'What's your name?'

'Mitchell.' He smiled at the two small figures who were like peas in a pod. 'But you can call me Mitch if you like.'

Georgia nodded, her red-brown curls dancing. Always a child of instant decisions, she now walked over to the figure sitting at the table before Kay could stop her, her voice loud as she said, 'Do you want to know how you can tell us apart so you don't get mixed up?'

Mitchell stared into the earnest little face. The child's tone had suggested she was doing him a great honour and his reflected he was fully aware of this when he said, 'Very much, please, Georgia.'

'I'm an inch taller than Emily and she has got some green in her eyes but mine are all brown, like Mummy's.'

'Right.' He nodded. 'Thank you, I'll remember that.'

Emily, not to be outdone, had now joined her sister at Mitchell's knee. 'My grandma has got some green in her eyes too,' she said importantly, 'and my Uncle Peter.'

'Have they?' Mitchell glanced at the two women for a moment before his gaze returned to the twins. All four faces were so alike it was almost comical, like three stages of life in one person. 'Well, you've both got very pretty eyes, your grandma and mummy too.'

The girls beamed at him and Kay realised she had to get a handle on this, and fast. 'Georgia, Emily, you go up with Grandma now and get changed out of your school uniform,' she said briskly. 'When you're washed and changed you can come down and have a glass of milk and a biscuit, okay?'

'Will you still be here?' Georgia asked Mitchell, without glancing in Kay's direction.

'I'm not sure.' The silver eyes passed over Kay's face, which now, far from being drained of colour, was burning hot. 'You'd better ask your mummy that.'

'Mummy—'

'*Georgia.*'

It was obvious the tone was one the twins recognised because they turned from Mitchell without another word, walking over to Leonora who had her hands outstretched for them and leaving the room with just a wave at Mitchell.

'They're delightful.' As the door closed he pre-empted what Kay had been about to say, following the statement by taking a huge bite of the carrot cake.

Kay stared at him, aware her face was on fire but unable to do anything about it as she said, 'Mr Grey, why are you here?'

'Mitchell, please.' It was soft, but carried a warning in the lazy tone. 'Unless you prefer Mitch, of course?'

'I don't prefer anything.'

He nodded, taking another bite of cake as though he had every right to sit at her dining table.

He was angry, furiously angry with her. Kay didn't know how she came by this knowledge because the hard, handsome face was to all intents and purposes relaxed and sociable, the unusual ice-blue eyes clear and inscrutable. She decided to take the bull by the horns. 'You're angry.' It was a statement, not a question. 'And I can understand that but it doesn't give you the right to come to my home like this.'

'I disagree,' he said, the conversational tone not fooling her for a minute.

She decided to try another tack. 'How did you get my address, anyway?' she asked hotly, forcing the aggression into her voice when really she was having a job to hide the trembling in her stomach.

Did she have any idea how young and vulnerable she looked standing like that, her whole stance one of hostility but her mouth and eyes betraying her panic and alarm? Damn it, she was looking at him as though he were some sort of monster. The thought increased Mitchell's fury rather than diffusing it. 'Obtaining your address was not difficult,' he said evenly. 'I had your name and telephone number, after all.'

'I don't want you here, distressing my mother and frightening the girls.' Even to Kay's own ears it sounded ridiculous. Her mother had clearly taken to him and he'd had the twins eating out of his hand.

'Then you shouldn't have bolted like a scared rabbit, should you?' he drawled with insufferable detachment. 'Surprising though it may seem, I didn't appreciate the position you put me in this lunchtime. Neither do I countenance the waste of good food,' he added indolently.

'You left me with no other choice,' she shot back.

'Forgive me if I don't see it that way.'

'I don't like bullies.'

'Neither do I,' he agreed, as though it had been an objective statement.

Kay glared at him even as she asked herself exactly what it was about this man that made her react with such uncharacteristic antagonism. She had no illusions about the male of the species, not any more, but until Mitchell Grey had come on the scene she had been able to handle them just fine. If nothing else, the last few years—when she had carved out a life and a career for herself, and become sole provider for her mother and the girls—had taught her she was more than capable of surviving without a man. And with that knowledge had come confidence and self-respect.

Mitchell finished the last of the cake, smacking his lips appreciatively as he said, 'Your mother's an excellent cook. It's been years since I had carrot cake, and I was starving.'

She didn't miss the innuendo in the last words but chose to ignore it. She had to get him out of here, *now*, and if an apology was what he'd come for it was a small price to pay to end this fiasco. Nevertheless, she found the words stuck in her throat. She swallowed, glancing at him as she searched for the right tone—cool, collected and not too penitent.

The blue eyes were tight on her, silver-bright and un-blinking, the corners of his mouth curved just enough in a cynical twist to tell her he knew exactly what she was thinking and what had motivated the forthcoming apology. It immediately withered and died. 'I'd like you to leave right now, Mr Grey,' she said crisply, her heart thumping painfully.

He folded his arms over his chest, settling more comfortably on the chair as he studied her interestedly—much as he'd done in the restaurant. 'I'm sure you would, Mrs Sherwood,' he said softly, the quiet emphasis on her name telling Kay her formal approach had been noted and was not appreciated. 'Tell me,' he continued, as though her demand had not been voiced, 'how did you leave the restaurant without my seeing you? I know it wasn't through the kitchens.'

Kay blinked. She'd half expected whoever had been sent to look for her would click onto what she'd done, but if he didn't know already there was no way she was telling him of her ignominious exit. She shrugged carefully. 'Does it matter?' she asked, forcing boredom into her voice.

'Do you know, I rather think it does—to me, that is.' His voice was low and rough now and for the first time Kay caught a glimpse of his outrage. It was immensely satisfying.

It was also an entirely inappropriate moment to feel amused but she couldn't help it, and although she kept her face straight it was clear he had sensed something when he said, 'Well? I'm not leaving until I receive the courtesy of an answer.'

Oh, to blazes with it! 'I climbed out of the washroom window,' she admitted expressionlessly.

There was a long moment of silence and then Mitchell began to laugh. Not a snigger or a sarcastic chortle, but a bust-a-gut roar of laughter that took Kay completely by surprise. She tried unsuccessfully to stifle her own amusement but his hilarity was infectious, albeit he was laughing at her, and she was still grinning when the silver-blue gaze swept her face again. 'I bet Harringtons had never seen anything like it before, and in that skirt,' he said, his voice still vibrating. 'You were fortunate not to do yourself an injury.'

She thought of her lacerated knees. 'Possibly.'

'And you would really rather dive out of a window than endure a lunch with me?' He'd stopped laughing now and something in his voice made the colour flare in her face.

'I... I don't like to be tricked,' she managed falteringly.

'And if you weren't tricked, what then?' he asked very softly, his voice oozing something that sent a tingle down her spine. He stood up as he spoke and she felt her body tense as he walked over to her, the overall height and breadth of him making her feel as small as the twins.

'I...told you, I don't date.' She wanted to take a step backwards but as he wasn't touching her it seemed silly, besides which she was worried it would give the wrong signals. She wasn't frightened of him, no way, she assured herself silently.

'Never?'

'Never,' she said firmly. 'There's the twins to take care of.'

'Your mother wouldn't babysit for one evening while

you go out?' he asked gently. 'I find that hard to believe.
She seems a very nice woman.'

'She is,' Kay said hotly, 'and of course she'd babysit
if I asked her but I choose not to. I prefer not to get
involved...' Her voice trailed away as the faint seductive
fragrance of his body warmth surrounded her. Kay's stomach clenched in protest at the tingles it was invoking. He
wasn't even holding her so how come she felt hot and
weak? she asked herself helplessly, a shiver of excitement
dancing over her skin.

'So do I.' He looked down at her, the black of his hair
throwing his tanned skin and mercurial eyes into even
more prominence. 'I thought we'd already established earlier we're two of a kind? Free, self-determining, autono-
mous.'

Kay stared into the strongly chiselled features. Men
were not to be trusted. They said one thing and meant
another, and when the another led to a desire to control
and subjugate the woman was fighting an uphill battle to
retain her individuality. Why, even her father—good as
he had been—had gambled with her mother's peace of
mind and security for the future and lost everything without even telling her what he'd been doing. Men were a
different species.

'I like women,' Mitchell said softly, 'but that doesn't
mean I'm prepared to walk into a snare or set one for
someone else. Fairy tales—one man, one woman and a
lifetime of for ever—are for children.'

'I don't—' She stopped, her cheeks burning. 'I don't
sleep around.'

'Good. Neither do I.'

'I meant—'

'I know what you meant, Kay.' He reached out and ran
one finger gently down her cheek, his touch feather-light.

She felt it in every fibre of her body. 'And I have no expectations, okay? I'm not a green callow youth who can only enjoy a woman's company if the end of the evening results in animal mating. Sex is more than that, it requires mental as well as physical stimulation and this is always better when a couple know each other and have built up a level of trust. One-night stands are not my idea of a good time.'

She didn't believe she was having this conversation. She had only ever slept with one man—Perry—in the whole of her life, and she had given him her body because he'd had her heart too. Mitchell was talking about something else entirely.

'I'm sorry.' Now she did take a step away from him, willing herself to puncture the seductive bubble he'd woven round them in the last minute or two. 'I meant what I said earlier. I don't want a relationship in any shape or form. I'm not ready to start dating again.'

He took her into his arms before she realised what he was doing, kissing her firmly but without undue force or roughness. She was rigid for a moment but, before she could struggle or object to the nearness of him, the delicious scent she'd smelt earlier and the feel of his body, hard and sure, wove a spell. She didn't actively respond, not at first; the sensations she was experiencing were too new and amazing for that, but as his mouth continued to caress hers, demanding greater and greater access, her body curved into his in unconscious pleasure.

She had never imagined in all her wildest dreams that a man could kiss like this, she thought dazedly. It was intoxicating, a sexual experience all in itself and as unlike anything Perry had ever done as chalk to cheese. Perry had kissed her only as a necessary preliminary to lovemaking, something to be moved on from swiftly to the real crux of the matter, but this...

His tongue rippled along her teeth before probing the inner sweetness of her mouth and her eyes opened wide in startled pleasure at the sensation it created, little needles of desire beginning to jab in her lower stomach. Her hands had been clenched stiffly against his chest but now they moved almost of their own volition to the broad shoulders, her eyelids closing in drugged enjoyment.

Her breasts were crushed against the wall of his chest, the slightest movement between them creating waves of pleasure radiating from their hard peaks, and she had to restrain herself from arching against him like a hungry cat.

'Kay?' As he moved her away from him to arm's length she opened bewildered eyes, staring at him as he murmured softly, 'I think the twins are on their way down.'

It was a drenching shock to realise she had been blind and deaf to the girls' approach when they burst into the kitchen a moment or two later, but in her customary inspection of two pairs of small hands before the milk and biscuits were served Kay pulled herself together.

'I'm glad you're still here.' Georgia's first words were for Mitchell. 'Have you finished talking to Mummy yet?'

'Yes, we're finished.' Kay answered her daughter before Mitchell could, her voice amazingly controlled considering how she was feeling inside. 'Now go and sit at the table, please.'

'Grandma says you're a friend of Mummy's,' Emily put in as she bounded across to the dining table after Georgia. 'Does that mean you'll come again?'

'Would you like me to come again?' Mitchell prevaricated, smiling into the two little faces that were so like their mother's.

'Yes!' They answered in unison.

'Then we'll have to see.'

Over her dead body. Kay smiled a tight smile before she said, 'Say goodbye to Mr Grey,' as she placed the two glasses and biscuits in front of the twins. 'I'll be back in a minute.'

She walked across to the kitchen door, opening it and waiting for Mitchell to precede her into the sitting room, which he did after one cryptic glance at her set face. Leonora was just descending the stairs, and as the older woman's eyes flew from her daughter's face to Mitchell's, and then back to Kay's, Kay said, 'Could you watch the girls a moment while I see Mr Grey out?'

'Certainly.' Leonora didn't remark that the twins were more than capable of drinking their milk and eating the biscuits without supervision, but what she did say was, and warmly—much to Kay's annoyance—'It was very nice to meet you, Mitch.'

'Likewise, and the carrot cake was wonderful.'

'Thank you.' Leonora dimpled and Kay felt like shaking her.

As Mitchell opened the front door and stepped outside Kay heard her mother shut the kitchen door with a very deliberate click, which spoke of her disapproval of her daughter's attitude. She gritted her teeth and then, as he turned to face her, said firmly, 'Goodbye,' before spoiling the curtness by adding—as the thought struck—'Where's your car?'

'Worried I might have to thumb a lift?' It was mocking. 'My chauffeur is parked round the corner and no doubt taking the opportunity to have a little nap,' Mitchell said softly. 'And before you ask, yes, I did make sure you wouldn't see the car when you came home. I thought you might bolt again.'

He made her sound like a temperamental pony. She glared at him, trying not to notice how daunting his height was.

'I'll pick you up at eight, by the way.' He had turned on his heel and was halfway down the garden path before her shriek made him noticeably wince.

'I'm not going anywhere with you tonight!'

He turned, a cool smile twisting his lips. 'Wrong,' he said silkily.

Was he mad or was it her? Because one of them must be. 'I thought I had made myself perfectly clear,' she said tightly.

'What you made clear, Kay, was that you need to be kissed,' he said with outrageous equanimity. She had also revealed—unwittingly but absolutely—that this ex-husband of hers had been the sort of man who took rather than gave. She might have the twins as proof that she was not unaccustomed as to what transpired between a man and a woman, but he would bet his bottom dollar that she was sexually unawakened.

He felt his body leap in response to the thought, hardening as it had done when he had held her. Was she freckled all over? he asked himself. He intended to find out. But he wouldn't rush her; she was as nervous as a cat on a hot tin roof as it was.

'I do *not* need to be kissed!' She had followed him halfway down the path, her voice a low hiss. 'And I especially do not want to be kissed by you.' Her voice was all the more adamant because she was lying to herself as well as him.

'Then I'll have to work on that,' Mitchell murmured thoughtfully. 'Every woman should want to be kissed.'

For goodness' sake! His skin must be inches thick, or perhaps it was just a giant ego that couldn't take no for an answer? 'That's such a typical male comment,' she said as scathingly as she could.

'There is nothing typical about me, Kay, as I intend to show you, but all in good time. For now I'm suggesting nothing more threatening than a good meal and a relaxed evening where you can unwind a little. You've obviously forgotten how to have fun but fortunately I know how to remedy that.' He smiled as if his words were perfectly innocent but she had seen the gleam in the back of his eyes. 'I'll pick you up later and don't bother to dress up, this place is very low-key. And before you object again—' he had seen her open her mouth in protest '—I'm not above using force to get my own way. Would you really like to upset the twins by letting them see their mother carried off kicking and screaming?'

'That's blackmail.'

'Dead right it is, and very useful at times.'

She glared at him, the last of the evening sunlight catching the red in her hair and turning it to living flame. 'You're despicable,' she ground out through clenched teeth.

'Like the song, "Baby, You Ain't Seen Nothing Yet".' He grinned at her, totally unabashed, and turned, striding off down the path and out of the gate without a backward glance.

Kay stood for some moments in the quiet of the evening, but apart from a dog barking in the distance somewhere and the sound of children calling to each other she heard nothing. Wherever he had stationed his car it wasn't close enough to hear the engine start.

She walked to the end of the path, leaning on the gate as she glanced up and down the quiet tree-lined street in which they lived. She had loved this street as soon as she had seen it; it was a higgledy-piggledy hotchpotch of houses, some small and some large, detached, semi-detached and even a small row of terraced Victorian houses at the very end of the road, and her tiny detached property sat right in the middle of it all.

Bruised and heartsore as she had been when she'd first come here, she had known instantly that the minute house was meant to be hers. It was tranquil, the whole street was tranquil and that was rare in this modern age. And now the tranquillity had been shattered! She frowned as the image of a hard, handsome face with eyes as cold as a moonlit sea flashed onto the screen of her mind. He'd had no right to come here, no right at all, but then she suspected Mitchell Grey was a man who took no account of right if it suited his purpose not to.

She moved restlessly as her heartbeat quickened at the thought. Why had she gone to his offices that day? Why couldn't it have been Peter or Tom who'd delivered the wretched document? She didn't want this, not any of it. He had said they were two of a kind but that was so untrue. He was as free as a bird but she had her precious babies to consider, and Georgia and Emily would always come first.

The dusk was thick now, the birds in residence in the trees overlooking the road jabbering in annoyance when a latecomer disturbed their bedtime. She stood for a moment more, trying to capture the feeling of peace and contentment she normally felt on such sojourns, but it was no good.

Sighing irritably, she turned back towards the house, glancing at her watch as she did so. Five o'clock. In three hours he would be here again, expecting her to go out with him. In spite of herself her pulse quickened. Well, she would go with him but she'd make sure she spelt out where she stood even more plainly than she'd done already. She was a mother, with commitments—not one of the carefree, sophisticated women of the world men like him favoured. And she didn't want to have 'fun', as he'd put it. She wanted...

Oh, she didn't know what she wanted, she admitted crossly as she pushed open the front door, but it wasn't Mitchell Grey.

If Kay had but known it, Mitchell's thoughts were very similar to her own as he sat in the back of his car, staring moodily out at the shadowed scene beyond the window as the big vehicle ate up the miles.

Why on earth had he pursued this thing once the mother had told him Kay had children? This just wasn't his scene at all. When had he ever had contact with tiny people? Never. He should have got out of there before she'd returned, but somehow he hadn't been able to bring himself to do that. But this was crazy—*he* was crazy. Damn it, she'd made it clear she wanted nothing to do with him.

He leant back in the seat, stretching his legs and shutting his eyes. What a fiasco of a day! He'd rescheduled the meeting with Jennings and postponed the visit to the docks at Southampton, which made the rest of the week damn awkward, and for what? A little slip of a redhead who wasn't even particularly arresting and came with the baggage of two offspring and a mother to boot.

But there was something about her... He shifted in the seat, opening his eyes again. He couldn't put his finger on it, but there was definitely something about her that was affecting him in a way he hadn't felt in a long, long time.

He shook his head, reaching for his briefcase and switching on the interior light as he pulled out a wad of papers that needed immediate attention. He would see her tonight and then make an end of it—decision made. He had an address book full of the numbers of women who would be only too pleased to spend an evening with him; Kay Sherwood was a complication he could do without. By this time next week he wouldn't even be able to remember what she looked like.

But he knew he was lying to himself...

CHAPTER FOUR

'YOU'RE not going out to dinner with Mitch dressed like that?'

Kay looked at her mother and sighed. The older woman had said very little about Mitchell's visit since he'd left, but her silence had spoken volumes, not to mention her enthusiastic conversation with the twins about 'the nice friend of Mummy's'. Now Kay said mildly, 'I'm *twenty-six*, not six, Mum, and more than capable of deciding what to wear. Okay?'

Leonora sniffed, gazing at Kay who had dressed after settling the twins in bed and had therefore just entered the sitting room. The black jeans and long-sleeved cashmere jumper in a pale shade of violet were obviously not to the older woman's taste.

'He said casual, remember?' Kay reminded her. 'We're probably dining at the local fast-food place for all I know.'

'Mitch would never take a date there.'

'How on earth do you know?' She was losing patience, Kay thought irritably, she really was. 'You've met the man for a few minutes, that's all. He could be a serial killer or died-in-the-wool bigamist or whatever—'

'Now you're being silly,' Leonora interrupted with another sniff.

'Mum, at the risk of destroying your illusions about the white knight on a charger you've apparently decided he is, the man is interested in one thing and one thing only,' Kay said vehemently. 'And as he's not going to get it

61

from me this is going to be a short and probably unpleasant evening. Let's leave it at that, shall we?'

'Oh, Kay.' Leonora walked across to take her hands, looking into her daughter's troubled face as she said, 'I just want you to be happy, that's all. You've had such a rough deal the last few years and a man like Mitch—rich, successful—'

'Single,' Kay put in mockingly.

'Yes, and single.' Leonora wasn't about to be put off by her daughter's sarcasm. 'A man like that only comes along once in a blue moon. Give him a chance, that's all I'm saying. See how it goes. Have some fun.'

'What is it about me that everyone wants me to have fun suddenly?' Kay smiled at her mother, her face rueful. 'Look, Mitchell Grey is just a ship that passes in the night, and by the end of this evening the term will be passed, I assure you. We have got absolutely nothing in common, for a start. He's rich, successful and single as you've just pointed out; we watch the pennies and come as a package or not at all. Not exactly the sort of bargain a man in Mitchell's position wants to strike. He could have his pick of any woman.'

'It's you he's asked out tonight,' Leonora pointed out swiftly.

'Maybe, but not in the way you think. More to prove a point after the episode at lunch.'

'Ah, but he asked you out to lunch, though, didn't he, in the first place?' It was triumphant. 'That must mean he's interested.'

'Don't hold your breath, Mum, that's all I'm saying, besides which I don't *want* a man. I'm perfectly contented with my life as it is.'

Leonora let go of Kay's hands without saying anything more but another eloquent sniff spoke for her.

'I'll leave my mobile on so you can contact me if you need me,' Kay said, glancing at the clock on the mantelpiece, which said five to eight. 'And if Emily starts coughing again her linctus is on the bedside cabinet. And no juice, if they ask for a drink—only water. I don't want sugar coating their teeth all night.'

'For goodness' sake just go and enjoy yourself, Kay,' Leonora snapped irritably. 'I'm more than capable of babysitting for one evening without you around, I do it often enough if you have to work a late delivery. You are supposed to have a life beyond that of mother to the twins, you know, dear as they are. You're young, you've still got your whole life in front of you. Stop acting as though you were my age.'

'Mum!' Kay was truly shocked and hurt and it showed.

Immediately Leonora retraced her steps, putting her arms round the younger woman and hugging Kay for a moment as she said, 'I didn't mean that the way it sounded, darling, really. I'm only thinking of you. You're a wonderful mother and daughter, the best there is, but it's time to put the past behind you.'

'I have,' Kay said firmly.

'I wish I could believe that.' Leonora had spoken pensively but then, as a knock on the front door announced Mitchell's arrival, the older woman started violently. 'He's here!'

Kay was amused to see there was something bordering on panic in her mother's face as she'd spoken, and it went some way to combating the butterflies in her own stomach. She breathed deeply before walking across the room and opening the door, and then her stomach turned right over as she looked into the dark face staring down at her. He looked sensational. The business suit had been replaced by a chunky black leather jacket and black jeans, which accentuated the brooding quality to his good looks even more, and she noticed he had shaved again, the five-o'clock shadow that had been evident earlier having vanished. For some reason the thought of him shaving because he was going to see her was so intimate it made her shiver—which only showed how dangerous it was to be around him, she warned herself silently.

'Hi.' He brought a big bunch of pale peach roses and freesias out from behind his back. 'These are for your mother.'

'Oh, right.' She was taken aback and it showed. He laughed softly, the silver eyes brilliant with mocking humour, and then she flushed pink as he delved in his pocket and produced a small transparent box in which reposed one delicate, beautiful white orchid.

'And this is for you,' he murmured, placing the box in her hands.

'Thank you,' she said uneasily. She didn't want him buying her anything. 'Come in for a moment while I get my coat.'

She left her mother gushing over the roses while she slipped upstairs for her jacket and took the opportunity to fix the dainty corsage on her jumper in front of the bedroom mirror, rather than give Mitchell the opportunity to suggest he do it for her. It had the most exquisite perfume, something resembling magnolia but slightly more exotic, and the smell was wafting under her nose as she went downstairs again.

Her mother and Mitchell were laughing about something or other as Kay descended, the atmosphere between them relaxed and friendly, and for a moment Kay felt thoroughly put out. It was almost as though he had inveigled his way into her life and home already, and she didn't like it. This was her refuge, her own tiny castle, but Mitchell seemed able to lower the drawbridge at will.

She smiled a brittle smile as they both turned to look at her, her voice tight as she said, 'Shall we go?'

'Sure.'

She noticed him raise his eyebrows at her mother in silent comment at the crispness of her voice but she pretended not to see. However, she did make a mental note to point out to her mother later that she had been right about the jeans. Mitchell was wearing them too. Admittedly his looked to be nothing short of Gucci or Armani, and hers were off the peg from one of the stores, but that wasn't the point.

'Where are you going?'

The three of them turned to see two small figures in teddy-bear pyjamas sitting halfway down the stairs, both sucking their thumbs and both with a rag doll tucked under one arm.

'Hey...' Kay's voice softened by several hundred degrees. 'What are you two doing up? You should have been asleep half an hour ago.'

'I'll see to the girls, you go.' It was clear Leonora was worried the best laid plans of mice and men were going askew.

However it was Mitchell who walked over to the foot of the stairs, smiling broadly at the two little girls as he said, 'I'm taking your mummy out for something to eat. Is that all right with you?'

They looked at each other and then turned back to him, nodding. 'We knew you were coming,' Georgia volunteered. 'We heard Mummy and Grandma talking about you.'

'Well, now you've said hallo I want you straight back into bed,' Leonora cut in hastily, moving past Mitchell as she added, 'Go on, right now, and I'll come and tuck you in.'

Kay glanced at Mitchell and saw his lips were twitching. He had obviously guessed whatever had been said wasn't particularly complimentary, but how could she have known the girls were listening? They had ears on them like donkeys, those two.

'Night night, darlings.' She called her goodbye as Mitchell turned and opened the door, but her mother was so intent on whisking the girls away before they said any more that she doubted they heard her.

'Was it that bad?' His deep, smoky voice didn't try to hide his amusement as they walked down the path.

'I'm sorry?' Kay prevaricated warily, although she knew exactly what he was asking. 'Was what bad?'

He glanced at her as he opened the garden gate and stood aside for her to precede him. 'I'm sure your mother is a wonderful woman,' he drawled lazily, 'but I doubt if tact is one of her strong points. Those poor kids' feet didn't touch the ground, she moved them so fast.'

'I'm sure I don't know what you mean,' she said primly, her voice a little weak as she stared at the magnificent sports car parked in front of the house. She didn't ask him if it was his car because it couldn't be anyone else's, but she was mentally blessing the fact she had decided to wear jeans and not a skirt as she looked at the low-slung monster.

He opened the passenger door and Kay slid into the leather-clad interior fairly gracefully, although she felt as though she were sitting on the floor, but when Mitchell joined her a moment later she felt every nerve in her body twang and vibrate.

'Put your seat belt on.'

'What?' She glanced at him and then wished she hadn't

because he was close, very close, and she was all of a dither as it was.

'Your seat belt?' He reached across her, the seductive and delicious smell of him adding to the sensations spiralling inside her and causing her heart to gallop. 'There.' Once she was strapped in he fixed his own seat belt before starting the engine, which purred into obedient life.

'Nice car.' She felt she had to say something to diffuse the electric atmosphere.

'Thank you.'

As the car leapt off with a low growl Kay just managed to stifle the squeak of fright, taking a deep breath before she said, 'What...what sort is it?'

'It's an Aston Martin sort,' he said softly.

'Oh.' She clearly should have known. 'I don't know much about cars.'

'There's no reason why you should.'

She *did* know that a car like this was a sex machine on wheels though, Kay thought desperately, and definitely a seduction tool in the hands of someone like Mitchell. She also knew from the one brief glance he was so close she only had to turn her head and move a little to caress that hard, square jaw with her lips... 'It...it must be quite expensive,' she managed weakly.

'Quite.' He spared her one piercing moment before his eyes returned to the windscreen. 'Boys' toys, is that what you're thinking?' he asked drily.

Boys' toys? There was nothing, absolutely and utterly nothing of the boy about Mitchell Grey. Kay tried to ignore the muscled legs and thighs clothed in black denim at the side of her. 'Not at all,' she said truthfully. 'Why? Is that how you view this?'

He smiled. 'Very cleverly sidestepped, Mrs Sherwood.'

Kay blinked. Had she been clever? She hadn't known she was being.

'Actually you might be right at that,' he continued quietly. 'I like fast cars with all the refinements, the thrill of speed and so on. I race at a private circuit now and then; you must come and watch some time.'

She couldn't think of anything she'd like less. 'Dicing with death?' she said coolly. 'I don't think I'd care to watch that. I think the gift of life is too valuable to be gambled on the turn of a card played by fickle fate.'

'Skill does play a small part in the proceedings.' It was very dry.

'Perhaps.' She shrugged. 'But if life is precious and happy enough, risking it in such a pointless way is not an option.'

His face didn't alter apart from his mouth tightening a little, but she knew he hadn't liked it. 'There are millions of people who would disagree with such a damning indictment.'

'That's their privilege,' she said shortly. 'It still doesn't alter what I think.'

'Are you seriously telling me that my participation in a sport in which I've been involved for many years is due to some kind of death wish?'

'I didn't say that.' She cast a sidelong glance at his grim profile. Wow, she'd *really* hit a nerve here. 'But I do think if you were utterly fulfilled in normal life you wouldn't need to take such unnecessary risks.'

'Spare me the amateur psychology.'

'Excuse me, but it was you who started this,' she said hotly.

Silence reigned for a few minutes as the car zoomed through the night at a speed Kay was sure was illegal.

'Why do you do that?' he asked suddenly, his voice rough.

'What?' She didn't have a clue what he was talking about.

'Argue, disagree, make waves,' he said irritably. 'No other woman I know is so damn opinionated.'

She bit down on the sharp answer that had sprung to mind and schooled her voice into order before she said evenly, 'If you want a dinner companion who will tell you exactly what you want to hear and agree with everything you say, as well as indicating she thinks you are a demigod who can do no wrong, you picked the wrong woman. I do have opinions and ideas of my own because I use the mind God gave me, and if you expect me to apologise for that or tread carefully in fear I might offend some precept of yours—tough. I've been in a state of mind where life lost its lustre and I know I could have taken chances then. Now is different. Life is precious now.'

'You're lucky,' he said drily.

'Perhaps. But luck is the flip side to misfortune and if you spin the coin fast enough both sides look the same. There were people who thought it was a calamity when I was left pregnant after Perry left—the final nail in the coffin—but it was the one thing in my life which proved a blessing and gave me strength to fight for the future.'

'Perry was your husband?' he asked softly, his swift glance taking in her intense expression.

'Yes.' She suddenly realised what she'd said and how much she had revealed, and to Mitchell Grey of all people.

'Don't freeze up on me again, Kay.'

Her eyes shot to the hard profile as his eyes turned to the windscreen again. 'I...I'm not,' she said shakily, dismayed at the ease with which he'd sensed her thoughts.

'So why did he leave?' he asked quietly.

He was aware she'd stiffened in the seat, but her voice came steadily when she said, 'I threw him out, actually. Her name was Tracy. But the marriage had been in trouble long before that. She...she was just the grand finale.'

'Do you still see much of him? What about the twins?'

'He's never seen them or been in contact since before the divorce.' When he made a sound deep in his throat she said fiercely, 'I like it that way, believe me. Look, can we change the subject?'

'Classical, rock or jazz?'

'What?'

'What type of music do you want on?' he asked patiently, making sure his voice revealed none of the anger that had gripped him towards this unknown husband who had let her down so monumentally.

There was a moment's pause, and her voice was a little shaky when she said, 'Jazz, please.'

Once the music was playing Mitchell concentrated on his driving and Kay sat quietly, her head whirling. She had been mad to tell him so much, she told herself bitterly. She should have kept the conversation light and easy, not spilled out everything barring her bra size! What must he be thinking? She stole a look sideways under her eyelashes but the granite profile was giving nothing away. Her throat felt locked and she couldn't think of a thing to say anyway, but the atmosphere inside the car was bordering on painful.

It was another ten minutes before he spoke, and then it was to say, 'We're nearly there, okay?'

She cleared her throat. 'Where's there?'

'Like I said, I thought we'd eat casual.'

Kay sat up straighter. There had been something in his

voice... 'Where's there?' she asked again, her voice firmer.

'My place,' he said evenly.

'Your place?'

'But don't worry, you won't be all alone with the big bad wolf,' he said mockingly. 'I have a housekeeper who's second to none and who provides a gourmet feast at the drop of a hat.'

Kay stared at him. 'Is she residential?' she asked at last.

'Of course.' His mouth twisted in the way she was beginning to recognise. 'I'm offering dinner, Kay, not bed and breakfast. I told you, I don't operate like that.'

She wasn't so naive as to believe there weren't men who said one thing and meant another; she'd married one, hadn't she? But it was too late now, she would have to make the best of this evening, besides which she didn't think Mitchell Grey was the kind of man who would force his attentions on a woman. He wouldn't have to, for one thing, she thought ruefully. They were probably queueing for the privilege.

It was just a minute or so before they turned off the main road they'd been travelling on and into a more dimly lit avenue, one where large houses were set in spacious grounds from what Kay could see, and it was right at the end of this road that Mitchell pulled up in front of two big iron gates set in a high stone wall. He opened the gates from the car by remote control, closing them again once they'd passed through, and now the beautifully landscaped gardens were lit here and there by means of small lights laced in the trees and larger ones discreetly hidden in flowerbeds and ornamental bushes.

The drive was a long one, and by the time Kay caught sight of the house some moments later she had realised it was set in the sort of lovely woodland setting most people would give their eye-teeth for.

She swallowed hard before she said carefully, 'What a lovely place. Have you lived here long?'

'Eight years.' He drew to a halt on the gravel drive in front of the house, turning to face her in the car as he draped one arm along the back of her seat. 'I got it for what the estate agent described as a 'song' at the time because it was filthy inside and neglected, and the grounds were just an impassable thicket beyond a boggy field. It had belonged to folk whose ancestors had once been the lord-of-the-manor type aristocrats, but for decades there'd been no money. The 'song' cost me every spare penny along with a hefty mortgage at the time,' he added wryly, 'but I gambled that the business was taking off and that within twelve months I'd be sitting pretty.'

Kay nodded. Narrow-waisted and lean-hipped as he was, his broad shoulders and considerable height made his presence all encompassing in the confines of the sports car, the dark magnetism at the heart of his attractiveness intensified a hundredfold. 'It clearly paid off,' she managed breathlessly.

Mitchell smiled. 'All that was needed was imagination, creativity, bags of energy and some tender loving care,' he said quietly, the last few words causing a fallout in her already jangling nerves. 'I did some of the work myself but it was the army of carpenters, builders, plumbers, gardeners and others who really made the difference. I decided I wanted to start off by enlarging the kitchen and adding bedrooms and bathrooms and went from there. Come and have a look round.'

Immediately Kay stood on the drive she was struck by the mellow silence. They could have been in the middle of the country for the lack of traffic noise.

They were only on the bottom of the circular stone steps leading from the drive to the front door when it opened to reveal a tall and distinguished-looking man, his white hair gleaming in the shaft of light from the hallway at the back of him.

'Mr Grey, I thought I heard the car.'

Mitchell didn't reply to this but what he did say was, 'Henry, this is the young lady I was telling you about, Kay Sherwood. Kay, meet my housekeeper, Henry.'

His housekeeper? She'd expected a buxom, bustling little woman for some reason, but the man in front of her was the epitome of an upper-class butler. And then this image was shattered somewhat when Henry said, his top-drawer voice holding a touch of glee, 'I'm very pleased to meet you, Mrs Sherwood. I've been waiting a long time to see a woman put Mr Grey in his place but I think you accomplished it magnificently this afternoon, if I may say so.'

'No, you may not, Henry.' In spite of the words Mitchell sounded mildly amused. 'Mrs Sherwood needs no encouragement from you, believe me.'

Kay hoped she didn't look as surprised as she felt. She wanted to glance at Mitchell standing at the side of her but resisted the impulse; instead, stretching out her hand to the housekeeper who was clearly a friend too, she said, 'Thank you for the vote of confidence, Henry. I'll try to live up to it.'

'I have no doubt you will, Mrs Sherwood.' Blue eyes were twinkling at her and as Kay stared into the good-looking face she saw Henry wasn't as old as the shock of white hair would have led her to believe. His face suggested he was somewhere around fifty or so, maybe fifty-five, but not much older, and his handshake was firm and dry. She decided she liked Mitchell's housekeeper.

'I'm going to show Mrs Sherwood round first, Henry, then we'd like cocktails in the drawing room.' Mitchell had obviously decided the tête-à-tête had gone on long enough because now he took her elbow, pressing her forward into the house.

Kay found herself in a high ceilinged entrance hall, the fine ash and oak panelling on the walls and light timber floor creating an immediate feel of light and spaciousness. And it was this same airy, stylish look, enhanced by strategically placed mirror and glass, gleaming timber and clean lines, that she found all over the large eight-bedroomed house.

The gracious drawing room with its muted background colours and clever use of texture and Indian wall hangings, the family sitting room, breakfast room, dining room and huge kitchen were all both graceful and modern, with strong richness of colour and warmth married to wood and aluminium.

All eight bedrooms were *ensuite* and each with their own individual colour scheme, but it was the enormous master bedroom in coffee and cream that caused Kay to feel distinctly uncomfortable. It was unashamedly masculine, the huge billowy water-bed the biggest she'd ever seen and clearly custom-made, and the stunning bathroom with its corner shower and whirlpool hydrotherapy bath unit, separate sauna and steam room, a sensual experience all in itself. Pictures of Mitchell lounging on the bed with some naked, voluptuous beauty or indulging in sinfully enjoyable skirmishes in the shower or bath positively cavorted in her head, and she was hot and breathless by the time he escorted her down to the drawing room again. And it made her thoughts all the worse, somehow, because Mitchell had behaved circumspectly throughout, his voice mild and pleasant as he'd shown her around, and his attitude cool and even distant. Whereas she...

Kay forced herself to breathe deeply and steadily as Henry served them cocktails in the drawing room, but she knew from his moment-too-long glance at her face that her cheeks were still burning, even before he said in an undertone to Mitchell, 'I'll turn the heating down a little, Mr Grey. And dinner will be served in twenty minutes.'

'Fine, Henry.' Mitchell sat back in his chair opposite Kay's, utterly relaxed and apparently at ease with the world. He seemed to feel no pressure to make conversation, Kay thought as she searched for a safe topic to take her mind off the big, lean body in front of her. He had discarded the leather jacket to reveal a midnight-blue shirt undone at the neck and open to reveal the first hint of a hairy chest, the blueness of his piercing eyes accentuated by the rich colour. He looked tough, brooding and infinitely male.

'You didn't say that Henry was a man.' As soon as she'd spoken she realised how silly it sounded, adding quickly, 'What I mean is, I thought your housekeeper would be a woman.'

He raised mocking eyebrows. 'In this day and age of sexual equality? Shame on you, Kay.'

She smiled stiffly in answer to the warm amusement in his eyes, utterly unable to relax. 'It seems as if you've known each other for a long time,' she tried again when he simply continued to lazily contemplate her without speaking.

'Ten years,' he agreed quietly. 'He was one of the best chefs in London then and earning a small fortune.'

She frowned slightly. 'Then why—?' She stopped abruptly, aware that he might misconstrue what she'd been about to voice.

'Why is he here working for me?' Mitchell finished for her, apparently not in the least put out. 'Long story.'

'We've got twenty minutes,' she persisted, suddenly immensely curious.

He surveyed her through narrowed eyes. 'The story's not mine to tell.' It wasn't unkind but very definite.

'You're friends.'

It was a statement not a question, but he answered her as though it were the latter. 'Yes, we're friends. Henry's an honourable man and I haven't met too many of those.'

Kay finished her cocktail. It was every bit as good as the Sweet Revenge. She looked over to the full-length windows, the drapes either side of them as yet not drawn. Beyond the windows a floodlit courtyard garden had been constructed, a timber platform having a section cut out to accommodate an overhanging magnolia. Stone slabs set in gravel, large rocks, wisteria, azaleas, together with a screen of weeping cherry trees and simple garden furniture completed the scene, which Kay thought must be wonderful at the height of summer.

Mitchell followed her eyes. 'It's very sheltered,' he said softly. 'I can often eat breakfast out there from early May to the end of October. Next time you must come in daylight; there's a tranquil spot by the lake you'd like, complete with resident ducks.'

'You have a lake?' she asked, ignoring the 'next time'.

'A small one,' he qualified lazily. 'We often barbecue down there in the summer, it's a sunny spot.'

'You really are the man with everything,' she said lightly, and she wasn't even sure herself if she was being nasty or just aiming to needle him.

'You disapprove of enjoying the fruits of your labour?'

'Of course not.' She might have known her attempt would fail, Kay thought as she stared at the faint amusement curling his mouth. 'But some people work hard all their lives and never have two pennies to rub together.'

'True.' He flexed his long legs, settling more comfortably into his seat, and her senses went haywire. 'But it's not in my power to rectify that,' he said logically.

He was making her feel like a recalcitrant child, the more so because he was reason itself.

'I enjoy having a base, somewhere that's totally mine,' he continued conversationally, 'probably because I never experienced that as a child. Even now I'm forever travelling here and there and spending the night in some damn hotel or other. This place is my citadel, my fortress.'

'It's a very lush fortress,' she said with a small smile.

'Whatever I do, I like to do well, Kay.'

She knew full well his words had a double meaning, but even if she had been fooled by his innocent voice the gleam in his eyes would have told her what he was thinking about. She refused to blush, however, her voice perfectly even when she said, 'A worthy attribute.'

'Isn't it?' he agreed gently.

'You didn't stay in one place for long, then, as a boy?' Kay had decided she couldn't win in open confrontation. That razor-sharp mind of his was always one step ahead.

'My father was an army man,' he said evenly, his whole persona undertaking a subtle transformation. He hadn't moved a muscle but suddenly the relaxed, easygoing soul had vanished and in his place was a hard individual with ice-cold eyes.

'And you and your mother travelled around with him?' She could see she shouldn't persist along this line—a blind man would have been able to see it—but she couldn't help herself. She had a burning and quite illogical—considering she was determined not to see him again—desire to know more about what made Mitchell Grey tick.

He nodded slowly. 'It made it difficult generally,' he said, a curious lack of expression in his voice. 'We never stayed for more than a couple of years in one place so putting down roots wasn't an option. New schools, new friends, new house, new district...' He shrugged. 'My sister and I didn't really have a sense of identity, I guess.'

'Your sister? You have a sister?' He hadn't mentioned her before; she'd thought he was an only child.

'Did have.' He stood up, reaching for her empty glass before walking across the room. 'She died in the car with my parents.'

'Oh, I'm so sorry, Mitchell.' He'd lost his whole family in one fell swoop and when he was still just a boy. Kay couldn't think of anything worse and her voice reflected her genuine horror and sympathy as well as her embarrassment that she'd pressed him. 'I shouldn't have asked.'

'Don't be silly, it was a long time ago, Kay.'

His voice was too controlled, almost flat, and revealed far more about how he really felt than she knew he would have liked. The accident might have occurred a long time ago but he wasn't over it, not by a long chalk. He had kept his back to her as he had spoken and as Kay stared at the tall, broad figure the urge to comfort him was so strong it shocked her. He was hurting, he'd been hurting for a long while but he'd never let anyone see, she realised with sudden intuition. She followed through on this last thought when she said softly, 'Did you have counselling after it had happened?'

'Counselling?' He had poured them both another cocktail and now he turned to face her, and she saw immediately his face was closed against her. 'I didn't need any mumbo-jumbo of that kind,' he said evenly. 'The accident had happened, they'd gone, and at times like that you can only rely on yourself to get through.'

'But you were just a boy—'

'I was fifteen years old, Kay, not a small child, and more than able to look after myself.' He had reached her side and now handed her the glass, adding, 'As it seemed you did after your marriage breakup.'

'That was different; I was a grown woman.'

'Oh, believe me, I'd been a man for years—' He broke off but not before Kay had glimpsed something raw in his face, something that stopped her breath. What on earth had gone on in his home for him to look like that? she asked herself silently. Whatever it had been it had affected the child Mitchell so badly it had crippled the man. One thing was for sure, the façade of cool, successful man of the world who had everything he wanted and who controlled himself and everyone else was just that—a façade.

She took a sip of her drink, her stomach trembling. She didn't want to go down this road, she told herself shakily, not with Mitchell Grey. While she could think of him as robot man—someone cold and ruthless and detached from normal life—she could keep him at a distance. This growing conflict within herself was not good. It was not good at all.

'Your mother told me how she came to be living with you and your children.' He'd reseated himself and it was clear he was changing the subject. 'It couldn't have been an easy time for you, your father dying so soon after the twins were born, but she said you were her rock.'

'Did she?' She hoped that was all her mother had said.

'You look too delicate and slender to be anyone's rock, but I'm beginning to understand that appearances are deceptive where you're concerned,' he murmured thoughtfully, his voice smoky rich again.

She could say she'd just been thinking the same about him, Kay thought wryly, but she wouldn't.

'It was a brave decision, to leave your job and flat and come back to take care of Leonora.'

Kay looked him in the eye. 'She'd have your guts for garters if she heard you put it like that,' she said drily, 'besides which it isn't really true. She went through a bad patch, admittedly, but there was no taking care of in any physical sense. She just needed us around and having to look after the twins while I worked was therapeutic. She's not weak,' she added as though he'd intimated it. 'She's a very strong woman at heart.'

'You must love her very much.'

'Of course I do.' She looked at him in surprise. 'She's my mother.'

'The two things aren't necessarily synonymous.' He stared at her with shuttered eyes as he drank.

There had been no inflexion in his voice to make her suspect he wasn't speaking generally, but she knew he was referring to his own mother. She swallowed hard. 'No, I guess not,' she said quietly before glancing round the drawing room and purposely making her voice light as she said, 'Do you know, I think the whole of the downstairs of my cottage would fit into this one room. You must be able to give some wild parties here.'

'Frenzied,' he agreed with a sexy grin, which made her breathing decidedly disjointed. 'Fancy coming to one?'

'When?'

'We could start right now, if you like. Two can party just fine.'

'That wasn't the sort of party I was referring to,' she reproved him firmly.

'Pity. They're by far the best kind.'

He slanted a wicked look at her under half-closed lids,

which was so hammed up Kay just had to laugh, even as she thought, He's like a chameleon, this man, with more personalities than I've had hot dinners.

'So, what do you normally do for relaxation?' he asked lazily, his eyes moving from the burnished curls tumbling about her shoulders, over creamy smooth skin before becoming fixed on her mouth.

Relaxation? Was that the few brief minutes between giving a hundred and ten per cent to her job, the twins, her mother and a hundred and one things besides? Moments that occurred rarely and usually when she was so tired all she wanted was a hot bath and an early night? Kay smiled coolly, pretending not to notice the way his eyes were stroking her mouth. 'This and that,' she said airily.

'Leonora said you don't go out nearly enough.'

She'd have a word with her mother when she got home! 'Really?' It was frosty.

'In fact she said you don't go out at all,' he said silkily.

'I told you before, I haven't got the time or the desire for romance,' she said, much too quickly.

'But the odd evening with a girlfriend at the cinema or the theatre isn't romance and you don't even do that,' he pointed out gently. 'All work and no play...'

Kay glared at him. How *dared* he lecture her on what she should do and what she shouldn't! What business was it of his anyway? 'Being a mother as well as the sole breadwinner does carry certain responsibilities,' she said starchily. 'Not that you'd know anything about that, of course. We can't all please ourselves and burn the candles at both ends.'

'You don't even get a light near the wick,' he said relentlessly, 'and it's really very bad for you, Kay. You owe it to the twins to be a well-balanced and rounded person.'

She couldn't believe her ears. 'You...you hypocrite!' To use little children in emotional blackmail.

'That's a harsh word,' he said sorrowfully, rising to his feet and placing his empty glass on the mantelpiece before walking over to her. 'Come here,' he said very softly, stopping just in front of her chair and holding out his hand to pull her up.

Her panicky heartbeat caused her breathing to become quick and shallow but she managed to sound reasonably firm when she said, 'No.'

He bent down, taking her half-full glass from her nerveless fingers and placing it on a small table at the side of the chair. She stared up at him, her eyes deep brown pools. He was going to kiss her again and it was only in this very instant that she admitted to herself how much she wanted him to. Nevertheless she made no movement when he held out his hand again.

'Kay,' he said, his tone steady but carrying the thread of warm amusement that made his voice sexier than ever, 'I'm only going to take you in to dinner.'

CHAPTER FIVE

'How did it go?'

Kay had hoped her mother would be asleep, considering it was one in the morning, but the moment she had gingerly opened the bedroom door Leonora's bedside lamp had been switched on. She glanced at the older woman as she walked across to her own bed, half amused and half exasperated by the bright anticipation in her mother's eyes.

'Okay.' She had undressed and washed in the bathroom where she'd had the foresight to leave her nightie before she went out, so now she slid under the covers, deliberately turning her face to the wall as she said, 'Goodnight.'

'*Goodnight?*' It was a low whisper in view of the twins asleep in the bedroom next door, but none the less intense because of it. 'Is that all you're going to say?'

'Mum, I've got to be up at six in the morning and my work schedule is manic. I've had a nice evening and now I'm home. All right?' Kay waited but the bedside lamp remained on. She pulled her pillow over her head with a low groan.

'Just one thing.' Her mother's voice was a subtle mixture of bribery and entreaty.

'What?' Kay didn't take the pillow away, her voice muffled.

'Are you seeing him again?'

The sixty-four dollar question. She wrinkled her face against it under the soft down, taking a deep breath before she said, 'No.'

'*Why?*' It was anguished.

'Because he didn't ask me, and that's two things,' Kay pointed out. 'Goodnight, Mum.'

She knew the effort it must have taken for her mother to say nothing more than a subdued, 'Goodnight, dear' as she switched off the lamp, but for the life of her Kay couldn't hold a post-mortem about the evening out loud. However, as she lay there in the darkness her mind was dissecting every moment from the second he had arrived to pick her up.

It had been a wonderful dinner. As she progressed to the meal her eyes opened in the blackness. And Mitchell had been an amusing and fascinating companion—as she was sure he had set out to be. She forced herself to lie still, aware her mother was still awake, but every nerve in her body was jangling as she recalled how he'd looked, what he'd said, the way he'd made her laugh in spite of her determination not to be charmed.

Each of the five courses—served by a smiling and courteous Henry—had been more delicious than the one before it, and the pièce de résistance in the form of a torrone mousse with oranges and strawberries had been the most spectacular dessert she had ever seen and tasted. She could see it now, decorated with a curl of chocolate, slices of strawberry and oranges, torrone and crystallised orange rind, and hear Mitchell's deep voice saying, 'Your eyes are as round as a child's in a candy store,' his tone soft and almost—her mind hesitated on the word—tender.

Oh... She turned over cautiously, colour flooding into her cheeks much the same as it had earlier.

They had lingered over coffee and brandy, talking about all sorts of things, and she'd had to keep reminding herself that this was Mitchell Grey, enemy, because it had been...what? She stared into the darkness. Great. Wonderful. Magical.

When he had called the taxi she'd known it was because he had been drinking, but at the back of her mind she'd thought he would make the most of the opportunity too. Right up until the minute she'd climbed into the back seat with him she'd told herself she wasn't going to let him kiss her again, but the second he'd reached for her she had melted against him like...like the flipping torrone mousse! Her hands clenched as she willed herself not to toss and turn.

She was an idiot, an absolute idiot, she belaboured herself miserably, her frustration at her own weakness compounded tenfold by the fact he hadn't asked to see her again.

The trouble was he was so *good* at the seduction game. The warm, masculine scent of him as he'd held her, his clean, warm skin and firm lips... She let herself drift into the recollection, her pulse quickening. He had kissed her as though he were delicately sampling something very sweet and costly at first, their lips touching and drawing apart, touching and drawing apart as he'd tentatively tasted and stroked her mouth into eager submission. When his kiss had gathered force she had been there with him every inch of the way, enchanted by the desire he'd been calling forth with consummate ease.

The caress of his mouth had become sensual, his lips and tongue invoking ripples of sensation into every nerve and sinew in her body, drawing her on to a place she had never been before. The shadowed darkness had enclosed them in their own little world of touch and taste and smell and he had pulled her into him so she'd been half lying across him, his mouth doing wonderful things to the sensitive flesh of her ears, her throat, the soft, silky skin over her collar-bone above the cashmere jumper.

She had known her control had been paper-thin and she didn't doubt he'd picked up the signs her body had been giving, so why hadn't he tried for more intimacy? Desire had dampened her skin and brought a throbbing ache in the core of her, but he had done no more than kiss and caress her. Of course they *had* been in the back of the taxi, but he hadn't so much as brushed her breasts on top of her clothes. Not that she wanted him to, of course, she lied vehemently. And she definitely did not want to see him again either, so it was just as well he hadn't suggested it. They had parted on relatively good terms—her skin burnt as she recalled the last lingering caress just before the taxi had drawn up outside Ivy Cottage—so that was a civilised ending to what had not been a civilised day in parts. One hand moved to her knees, which were tight and sore.

And now she had to get some sleep. She breathed slowly and deeply, consciously shutting off her whirling thoughts as she employed a technique she'd perfected during the last caustic months with Perry and the ensuing aftermath. It took longer than usual but eventually she fell into a deep and dreamless slumber, curled under the duvet like a small, solitary animal.

The next morning bedlam reigned, as it so often did in the mad rush to get the twins dressed, fed and ready for school and herself out of the house by eight o'clock, but when Peter pipped his horn outside the cottage gate Kay was ready.

'Hi.' Her brother's greeting was distracted but that wasn't unusual; he'd never been much good in the mornings. Kay welcomed this today, it meant he'd probably forgotten all about her lunch with Mitchell the previous day and so she needn't go into the whole wretched story. She normally rode to work on her motorbike and Peter and Tom had a van each, but the bike had needed an overhaul and so she was picking it up at the garage near the office first thing.

'Hi yourself.' She settled herself into the seat beside him. She was already dressed in her leathers and intended to go straight to the first job from the garage. 'I'm out all day but there are a couple of breaks for both you and Tom in the schedule; make sure you check the answer machine as soon as you get back to the office, won't you? And of course any new deliveries you can fit in today take on, and don't forget to write everything down.'

'Sure thing, boss.' Peter spared her a fleeting grin before pulling away into the traffic.

'We're going to have to get someone in to man the phone if nothing else,' Kay mused out loud as the van sped along. 'With all the work we've got I'm rarely in the office these days, and it would be great for someone to be in charge in there and do some of the day-to-day paperwork. I'm so behind with it.'

Peter nodded. 'Talking of all the work we've got, how did your meeting with Mitchell Grey go?' he asked casually. Too casually.

Kay stared at him. 'Mum phoned you,' she said flatly.

'Well, not exactly, it was more... Yes, she did,' he admitted wryly, keeping his eyes on the traffic ahead.

She might have known! There were times when she felt she was living her life in a goldfish bowl. 'So? What exactly did she say?' She tried, and failed, to keep the annoyance out of her voice.

'Just that the lunch hadn't gone too well—something about you having jumped out of a window,' Peter said, as though such an occurrence were perfectly normal—and that he'd turned up at the house and you were seeing him last night.'

'That about sums it up,' Kay said shortly.

'Any business coming our way from him?' It was hopeful.

'No.'

'Right.'

The rest of the journey to the garage was conducted in silence.

By the time Kay drew up outside Ivy Cottage at six in the evening she was bone-tired. The day had gone well without any hitches, the weather had been kindness itself—mild, sunny with a positively warm breeze—and she'd had plenty of time for a snack at lunch time plus a couple of coffee breaks during the day. So why, she asked herself as she wearily parked the bike at the side of the house and pulled off her crash helmet, did she feel as if everything was wrong? It wasn't like her.

She flexed her aching neck muscles, looking up into the dark evening sky as she did so. It was Halloween in a day or two, then Guy Fawkes night and before you knew it Christmas would be upon them and the end of another year would be fast approaching. And it had been a good year. The business had grown, the twins were well and happy and had taken to big school like ducks to water. Her mother was settled and comfortable in her mind again, and Peter and his family were financially secure after finally paying off the last of the debts that had accumulated during the time her brother had been out of work, before she'd started Sherwood Delivery.

So—everything positive and nothing negative. Moonlight lay in silver pools in the garden and someone somewhere had lit a bonfire earlier, the smell of wood smoke drifting in the breeze and adding to the perfection of an English autumn evening. Stars sparkled above, the last of the dying leaves on the trees whispered below— *and she couldn't stop thinking of Mitchell Grey*. It was a relief to finally admit it to herself.

Kay lowered her head, staring blindly into the sleeping garden as the faint sounds of a television and children's laughter from within the house brushed over her.

What was it about him that had so got under her skin? she asked herself silently. She knew there wasn't one single thing going for any sort of relationship between them, and they were as far apart as east was to west, so why had he been there in her head for every second of every minute of the day?

Was it just the dizzying and lethal combination of fascination and danger? Or the sexual magnetism he exuded like no other man she had ever come into contact with? Or the potent aphrodisiac of wealth and success and power?

She leant back against the wall of the house, taking a deep lungful of sweet smoky air. Whatever, she was in a spin and she had never felt like this before, alive from the top of her head to the soles of her feet—tinglingly, frighteningly, thrillingly alive.

'Stop it.' She actually spoke the words out loud, needing to hear them. 'Stop this right now. It's over, finished, not that it ever really began. You were just an irritating hiccup in his busy life, that's all. He didn't ask to see you again, which is just as well. You are a mother of two children, not exactly the sort of woman Mitchell Grey would go for.'

She took a few more lungfuls of air before straightening her shoulders and raising her chin.

It would be dangerous to get mixed up with him, very, very dangerous; every instinct in her body was telling her so. And with Georgia and Emily relying on her to be both mother and father, danger was not an option. Everything had worked out for the best and these ridiculous feelings would soon shrivel and die. They would have to.

She marched round the side of the house to the front door, opening it and stepping into warm light and the delicious smell of one of her mother's pot roasts—that and the sweet perfume emanating from the most gigantic basket of flowers set at an angle on the coffee-table to catch her eye as soon as she came in.

'Kay! Hallo, darling.' Her mother appeared from the direction of the kitchen at the same time as the twins jumped up from the sitting-room carpet where they had been lying in their pyjamas playing a board game together.

'Mummy, Mummy, look!'

'Mummy, we've been waiting for you to come home for *ages*.'

They had seized her hands, pulling her over to the basket of flowers, their small faces alight, and over their heads her mother mouthed silently, Mitch?

'There's a card, Mummy, but Grandma wouldn't let us open it.' Georgia was hopping from one foot to another in an agony of anticipation. 'Look, there.'

Kay obediently extracted the small envelope from the profusion of cream and yellow rosebuds, carnations, orchids, daisies and freesias, hoping her mother wouldn't notice her hands were trembling. It was addressed, 'Mrs Kay Sherwood, Ivy Cottage, 24 Bishops Road'. She stared at it for a moment before turning it over and carefully slitting the top open. The small card inside read, 'I enjoyed last night. Can we do it again some time? M.'

She read it twice and then handed it to her mother who was at her elbow, before turning to the twins and saying, 'It's a present to all of us from Mr Grey, the gentleman you met last night? Isn't that kind of him?'

'For us too?' Georgia and Emily were enchanted.

'For all of us,' Kay repeated firmly. *'Can we do it again some time?'* What did that mean? Was this an extravagant brush-off or did he really mean to contact her? And if he did, what was she going to do? It would be utter folly to see him again; it would give all the wrong signals. But perhaps this was how he always gently let a woman down? She had no idea of how men in his position of wealth and influence behaved.

She glanced at her mother and the older woman's eyes were waiting for her. 'They're beautiful flowers,' Leonora said impassively, handing Kay back the card as she spoke.

'Yes, they are.'

'And there's so many of them,' Leonora pointed out.

'Yes.' She stared at her mother and Leonora stared back.

'I'll see to our dinner while you shower and change. The girls have already eaten but I said they could stay up a while, okay?'

'Yes, fine,' Kay agreed quickly. Anything to prevent a cosy chat over dinner.

She asked the twins about their day and admired some paintings they had brought home from school for her before going upstairs, angry with herself for the excitement bubbling in her veins. She had to get a handle on this, she told herself, stripping off her clothes in the bedroom and padding through to the bathroom in her robe. She hardly recognised herself any more.

Once in the shower she let the warm water wash the tension away, standing under the flow for longer than usual. She thought she heard the telephone ring at one point but, when no one called her, assumed the call was one of her mother's friends.

By the time she had dressed in a light jumper and old jeans she felt more like herself again. She stared at the face in the mirror. Her freckles seemed to stand out even more tonight and she was sure she was getting a pimple on her chin. Mitchell Grey interested in her, indeed! She must have been mad. But no more, she was quite sane again. The flowers were his way of saying goodbye. He could have asked to see her again last night if he'd been interested, or written something specific on the card.

Her mother called to her from the kitchen as Kay walked downstairs. 'There's a sherry by the sofa for you, and one for me. I'll come and join you in a minute.'

'Thanks.' Kay sat down and immediately Georgia and Emily climbed either side of her, snuggling into her like two small puppies. She stroked their curls, still damp from their evening shower and smelling of baby shampoo. Her precious babies, how could she want more from life than having them close to her? she asked herself guiltily. And she didn't, not really. *She didn't.*

The phone rang and her mother appeared like the genie from the lamp. 'That'll be Mitch,' Leonora said casually. 'He called earlier when you were in the shower. I told him to call back in a few minutes.' She didn't meet Kay's eyes as she spoke.

Georgia had already lifted the receiver, speaking the number as Kay muttered, 'Mum!'

Then the little girl said brightly, 'Yes, Mummy's downstairs now,' holding out the phone as she called, 'Mummy!'

Kay's heart had begun a wild hammering, the palms of her hands suddenly damp. She stood up, walking over to

Georgia and taking the phone from the little girl as though the receiver were red hot. 'Hallo,' she said weakly.

'Kay? This is Mitchell.' It was soft, darkly seductive, and she shivered.

'Mitchell?' She hoped her voice sounded stronger than she felt. 'Thank you so much for the flowers; they were a lovely surprise but you really shouldn't have.'

'My pleasure.'

His cool, easy tone made a mockery of her racing pulse and Kay made a huge effort to pull herself together.

'I was wondering if you're free at the weekend?'

'I...um...' She had never felt so confused in her life. If she said no he probably wouldn't bother again; if she said yes...

'I thought maybe dinner and a film on Saturday evening? Or we could just go for a drink somewhere if you prefer?' His voice gentled still further as he added, 'No big deal, Kay, that's what I'm saying. You said you're not ready for a relationship; I think you need to be let out of the steel box you've put round yourself and start testing life again. So we start as friends with no strings attached and go nice and slow. Any time either of us wants out, that's fine. Any time either of us wants to take it a step forward we discuss it. How's that?'

Cold-blooded in the extreme. Kay stared blankly across the room. He was talking with about as much emotion as he would when suggesting a business deal. She didn't know whether to be pleased by his reasonableness or offended by the lack of ardour.

'Kay?'

His quiet voice reminded her she couldn't hesitate any longer. She took a deep breath. She had to admit he couldn't have been fairer and this way she had nothing to lose. 'A meal and a film sounds great,' she said carefully.

'Good. I'll pick you up at seven and book tickets for a late performance. Anything in particular you'd like to see?'

It dawned on Kay afresh just how much of a rut she was in when she realised she didn't have a clue what films were out. She hadn't been to the cinema since the twins were born. She'd hardly been *anywhere* since the twins were born! 'You choose,' she said hastily.

'I'll surprise you,' he said softly.

Kay swallowed. 'Fine.'

She was sure his voice was redolent with amusement when he made his goodbyes, but as her mother was positioned in front of her now she didn't prolong the farewell.

'You're seeing him again.' Leonora spoke as though Kay had won a gold medal at the Olympics.

'Calm down, Mum. It's strictly on a friends-only basis,' Kay warned softly, vitally aware of her daughters' little faces as they stared up at her.

Leonora smiled benignly. 'Of course it is.'

Kay stifled the words hovering on her tongue, instead saying, 'I'll talk to you later, okay? Once we've eaten.'

'As you like, dear.' Leonora sailed off back into the kitchen, every inch of her still-slim body registering satisfaction.

Wonderful. Kay stared after her mother, frustration paramount. What was it about Mitchell Grey that could charm any female within a ten-mile radius? she asked herself irritably.

'Was that the man who sent those?'

Emily had spoken, her dimpled hand pointing to the basket of flowers as she stared at her mother.

Kay nodded. 'Yes, it was, sweet pea.'

'I like him.'

'So do I,' Georgia agreed earnestly.

Kay plumped down on the sofa, her hand reaching for the sherry glass. Three against one wasn't really fair, was it?

CHAPTER SIX

THE next few weeks were ones of change. Kay found herself seeing Mitchell every day; they ate lunch or dinner together, sometimes in one of the plush restaurants Mitchell frequented or at his home, they danced in nightclubs, visited the cinema and theatre, went bowling, ice-skating and even scoured one or two antique fairs and auctions. As he had promised they had fun—lots of fun. But it wasn't really *real*, it wasn't everyday life. Not her life, at least, Kay reflected.

She was standing in the kitchen on the Saturday morning before Christmas, up to her elbows in suds, idly watching the garden's resident robin as he militantly sent off one or two marauding sparrows who had thought to plunder the bird table of pieces of bacon fat.

If she thought about it, they hadn't had one no-holds-barred conversation since that first evening at his home. Oh, he had entertained her all right, and, yes, if she was totally honest, the more she saw him, the more she liked him, but... She frowned at the window. She didn't know him at all. He was tough, formidably in control of himself and those around him, but she could never penetrate that invisible barrier even in the slightest. And the ironical thing, the really *ridiculous* thing was that he'd accused her the night before of the self-same thing.

'What will it take before that barricade is smashed?'

She had glanced at him as he'd spoken, his voice soft and his eyes faintly amused as they'd driven home after a night at the theatre.

'Sorry?'

'You know what I mean, Kay.'

His tone had still been easy, even lazy, but perhaps—in hindsight—there had been something more, anger even, behind the indolent posture.

'I don't.' She'd tightened instinctively.

He had said nothing for a mile or two, handling the car with his normal expertise, and then he had made some fatuous remark about the play they'd just seen, one that hadn't necessitated an answer but that had made a reluctant smile come to her lips. And so the moment had passed.

His goodnight kiss had left her aching for more, as his kisses always did, but again—analysed in the cold light of morning without the normal unbearable sexual tension sending her into a spin—she felt he had been playing a part. So far but no further, mentally, emotionally and physically, that was how she felt it was. But then, was she really any different?

She shut her eyes tightly, biting on her lip as she washed a breakfast plate with unnecessary vigour. He unnerved her more now than when she had first met him, that was the truth of the matter. The more she was with him, the more she wanted to be with him, and that wasn't how it was supposed to have been.

Maybe if they had gone to bed, if they'd become lovers in the full sense of the word, this crazy attraction would have burnt itself out? And then she curled her lip at the stupidity of the thought. It might well have on his side, in fact she didn't doubt it for a minute, but she wasn't built like that. The reason she had tried and tried for her marriage to work even when logic had said it was doomed was because she'd committed her body as well as her heart. The two were inseparable where she was concerned. It might not be the prevailing fashion but she couldn't help that. She couldn't bear the thought of being just another notch on his bedpost, figuratively speaking of course, she added, thinking of the massive water-bed as she smiled wryly.

Kay flexed her shoulders, which had become tense with the nature of her thoughts.

Had she been wrong in keeping any contact between Mitchell and the twins to an absolute minimum? she asked herself soberly. Had that added to the contrived, meretricious nature of it all? One minute she was being dined and wined in the most fabulous of places or being whisked off to goodness knew where with money no object, the next she was back home changing the girls' beds in the middle of the night when they'd succumbed to the stomach bug playing havoc at their school, or checking their thick curls in response to a letter from the nurse who'd warned parents a child in their class had been found to be lousy.

The thing was, she hadn't wanted Georgia and Emily to get used to Mitchell, to get fond of him, she admitted reluctantly. It wasn't fair on them. He had made it plain on that first date that long-term fidelity wasn't an option, and she'd known that this friendship that wasn't a friendship but defied any label she could think of wouldn't last. But how could you explain that to two little girls who had been determined to like him from the first?

She sighed heavily, finishing the washing-up and drying her hands on a towel before she boiled a kettle for the lemon drink she was making for her mother. Leonora had been suffering from what she'd insisted was a cold the last couple of days, but this morning the older woman had been too ill to get out of bed and Kay had called the doctor. She suspected her mother had fallen foul of the vicious flu bug that was sweeping the country, but the hacking cough that had become much worse during the night spoke of a chest infection on top of the virus.

Kay was just at the bottom of the stairs with the mug of hot lemon when a knock at the front door announced Dr Galbraith.

The doctor was cheerful enough as he examined Leonora, but once downstairs in the sitting room he lowered his voice after glancing at the twins—snuggled together watching a Christmas cartoon in front of the fire—and said quietly, 'We need to watch that chest infection. I don't want it developing into anything more serious, so don't take any nonsense from her about getting out of bed. A side effect of this particular virus is inflammation of the lungs in my more elderly patients, not that your mother would appreciate being referred to in that regard,' he added with a wry smile. 'Plenty of liquids along with the antibiotics and paracetamol, all right?'

'Thank you, Doctor.' Kay nodded and then wished she hadn't as the headache she'd woken up with made itself known.

'You look a bit peaky yourself,' Dr Galbraith said as he took in her pale face, the whiteness of her skin in sharp contrast to her red curls. 'You might be going down with it—it does tend to run through a whole household. Get plenty of paracetamol in and call the surgery if you need to. Frankly, if you'd got anything planned over Christmas I'd cancel it now.'

Great. And a happy Christmas to you too! 'Thank you, Doctor,' Kay repeated, and saw him out into the frosty morning, shutting the door quickly as the icy chill made her shiver.

'Shoes, coats and hats, girls,' she said with deliberate brightness, knowing the twins wouldn't appreciate being pulled away from their Saturday morning programmes on the TV. 'We've got to go and get some medicine for Grandma, and if you're good we might call in the cake shop and buy two of those gingerbread men you like so much.'

Fortunately the row of shops comprising a small supermarket, chemist, cake shop, butcher's and grocer's was only a couple of streets away, but nevertheless Kay was regretting she hadn't had one of the vans for the weekend by the time she and the girls got home later that morning. She was feeling worse by the minute and now Emily was complaining her head hurt her, and refused to eat her gingerbread man, which she normally loved.

After remaking her mother's bed and giving Leonora the antibiotics and paracetamol with another hot lemon drink, Kay went downstairs to find Emily lying listlessly on the sofa with her teddy bear. When her daughter refused a chocolate off the little Christmas tree standing next to the TV, Kay knew she was ill, although Georgia was bouncing around as usual.

She felt the small forehead, alarmed to find it was far too hot, and in bending over nearly landed on top of Emily when she went all giddy. Darn it, they were dropping like flies and Christmas was only three days away, and the girls had so been looking forward to it.

Emily tucked up in a blanket in her pyjamas on the sofa after a dose of paracetamol for her temperature, Kay made herself a fortifying cup of tea and took stock. Fortunately she'd made the decision to close the office all the following week as Christmas day was on the Tuesday, so work wasn't a problem. They had enough food to last them for a while, although she had been going to do the big Christmas shop on Monday—still, she might feel better by then, and she could perhaps call Peter in to sit with the girls while she went out. No, that wouldn't do. She didn't want to infect Peter and his family for Christmas. Oh, she would manage somehow; she couldn't think of that now with her head aching so badly.

Mitchell. She sat up straighter in the kitchen chair. She had been going to go out with him this evening; she must call him and explain.

It was Henry who answered the telephone, but within moments Mitchell's deep rich voice said, 'Kay? Henry said your mother isn't well?'

'It's the flu along with a chest infection, and now Emily is feeling poorly. I'm sorry but I can't make tonight.'

There was a pause, and then he said, 'How would it be if I hired a babysitter? I know a couple of my friends swear by a certain—'

'No.' She didn't let him finish. She would no more have let a stranger—however well recommended—babysit her girls than fly to the moon. 'I'm not feeling too good myself, actually, so we'd better leave it.'

Another pause, and then he said evenly, 'This isn't because of last night, is it?'

'What?' She didn't have a clue what he was talking about.

'I have a feeling the drawbridge is being raised,' he said softly, 'rather than the barriers coming down.'

Why did men think everything was about *them* all the time? If she had been feeling better she would have let rip; as it was she just said quietly, 'Mitchell, my mother is ill in bed, my daughter has a temperature and I don't feel great myself. Those are the facts, okay? I'll ring you.' And she put the telephone down. She couldn't argue with him, not today. He'd have to think what he liked.

The telephone rang almost immediately and she breathed deeply and braced herself before picking it up.

"Kay, if you need anything give me a call." It was

Mitchell, his voice holding a quality that suddenly—ridiculously—made her want to cry.

'Thank you.' She managed to keep the wobble from sounding. 'We'll be all right, but thank you.' And then, as Emily chose that moment to reach out for her glass of orange juice on the small table Kay had pulled close to the sofa, catching it with the teddy bear's foot as she did so and sending the glass and its contents cascading onto the floor, she said, 'I have to go. Goodbye, Mitchell,' and she put down the phone on his soft 'Goodbye.'

That night Kay was up and down to Emily several times as well as helping her mother to the bathroom twice, Leonora being too weak to stand by herself. Kay knew she was going down with the flu now—her headache was blinding, she was cold and shivery but her skin was clammy to the touch, and everything was a huge effort. By morning she felt so ill she didn't know how she was going to cope, and she just prayed Georgia wouldn't get sick.

The morning passed in a haze of fixing hot drinks, dispensing medicines and checking Emily's temperature, and when the telephone rang downstairs as she was staggering to the bathroom with Emily in her arms Kay felt too exhausted to even call and ask who it was when she heard Georgia talking to someone.

She was tucking Emily back in bed when Georgia appeared at her side. 'That was Mitchell,' Georgia said importantly. 'I said everyone was poorly except me, and he said I've got to help you. What shall I do?'

Kay lay down on Georgia's bed, next to Emily's, for a moment or two as the room spun. 'Just be a good girl,' she whispered weakly, 'and play with your toys until I get your lunch in a minute.'

She was aware of Georgia nodding and then scampering out of the room, and she shut her eyes, willing the dizziness to pass. It seemed like the next second when she heard voices downstairs but she knew she must have been dozing. She forced her leaden limbs to obey her, sitting up and then swinging her legs over the side of the narrow bed before she rose and tottered towards the door. She was hanging onto the door knob like grim death, the landing a kaleidoscope of rotating colour when a deep voice said, 'What the...?' a moment before she felt herself lifted right off her feet.

'Mitchell.' Kay was aware she was clutching at him but the dark face above hers was barely in focus. 'I feel so ill.'

Leonora was calling from the other bedroom, obviously wondering what was going on, and now Kay said frantically, 'She mustn't get out of bed; she'll fall and hurt herself.'

Mitchell didn't answer this except to shout, 'Henry! Get up here,' making Kay wince as the sound reverberated in her brain and made it rattle.

She heard Mitchell tell Henry to go and reassure her mother everything was all right—although what her mother would make of a strange man entering her bedroom, Kay didn't know—but with Mitchell here taking charge she suddenly felt so utterly helpless, so weak and drained, it was too much effort to keep her eyes open. He was holding her next to his chest, his strength and vitality tiring in itself, and then she felt herself placed on Georgia's bed again and he said, 'Lie there, Kay, and don't move. I'm going to have a word with Leonora,' just before he added, 'It's okay, little one, Mummy's just a little sick like you,' as Emily began to cry.

Kay struggled into a sitting position, holding out her arms as she said, 'Pass her to me, Mitchell, please.'

She sat cradling Emily to her as she heard voices in the bedroom next door but it was too much effort to try and distinguish what was being said. If Mitchell would be prepared to stay for just an hour or two so she could sleep a while she would be all right, Kay told herself. It was the combination of a sleepless night on top of the flu that had knocked her for six.

She came to with a start a little while later, staring bleary-eyed at Mitchell, who had just marched into the room. 'Everything's settled,' he said briskly, reaching down for Emily who was fast asleep on Kay's lap. 'You're coming home with me.'

'What?' She was still in one of the weird catnap dreams she'd been having since the flu hit; she had to be. He couldn't really have said what she'd thought he'd said.

She saw him hand the still-sleeping Emily to Henry, who had appeared in the doorway, and then he turned back to her, saying, 'Georgia and Emily will need a couple of changes of clothing and their night things. Where are they?'

'Mitchell.' She struggled to get the words past the cotton wool in her head. 'I'm not going anywhere. What are you talking about?'

'I'm taking you all to my place.' It was not an invitation, more of a decree.

'No way.' She wasn't *that* ill. 'I've far too much to do here for Christmas.'

'Christmas has been moved.' He eyed her impatiently. 'All the presents you and your mother had hidden from the twins are in the back of my car concealed under a blanket. There's also some of their toys from their toy boxes so they've got something to play with over the next couple of days. Once we've packed their clothes we're done.'

Done? *Done?* Was he mad? 'My mother, our clothes...' she said weakly.

'All in the car.'

'You've put my mother in your car?' she said faintly.

'Not in the boot with the other things,' he qualified with dry amusement at her horrified tone.

If she hadn't have felt so rotten she would have glared at him. 'Her pills—'

'I've told you, all taken care of,' he said with the touch of irritation she'd noticed on other occasions when he considered she was labouring a point. He had walked across to the twins' wardrobe as they'd been speaking, opening it and taking various clothes, underwear and night attire from the hanging space and shelves inside. 'That'll do.' He put the mound on Emily's bed. 'Where's a suitcase?'

'There's a big sports bag on top of the wardrobe,' she answered in a whisper, her throat hurting badly. She couldn't argue with him, she didn't have the strength, but she couldn't believe this was happening, and with her mother's consent too. Consent? She dared bet her mother nearly bit his hand off, so quickly did she agree to Mitchell's offer. They'd certainly tied it all up tight while she'd been dozing.

'I'll take this bag to the car and come back for you,' he said quietly, looking down at her with unfathomable eyes once the clothes were packed.

'We...we surely can't all fit in,' she murmured.

'I came in the Voyager,' he said briefly.

'Oh, right.' She didn't know he had one. He seemed to have a vehicle for every occasion, she thought with a slight touch of flu hysteria as he left the room.

It was only when she heard his footsteps going down the stairs that it dawned on Kay he must have planned to take them back to his place all along if he'd brought the huge people carrier. She wasn't quite sure how that made her feel but now was not the time to explore her emotions, she told herself muzzily. She made a great effort and got to her feet, her legs feeling as if they didn't belong to her.

She was halfway down the stairs when he came in the front door and he swore, softly but a very rude word, she thought primly.

'What are you trying to do, Kay? Prove a point by breaking your neck?' he grated out angrily, glaring at her as she wobbled on the last step.

'Don't shout at me,' she muttered weakly. 'I'm not one of your female slaves who only live to do your bidding.'

'I wish.' He shook his head at her as she clung to the post at the bottom of the stairs. 'Look at you, dead on your feet and still determined not to give an inch. Superwoman is allowed to be ill, you know. Even the most magnificent of the species have off-days.'

'Probably.' The room was swimming again and she was forced to acknowledge the brief few steps had taken all her strength. 'But if I don't look after Georgia and Emily and my mother no one else will.'

'Wrong.' He picked her up as though she weighed nothing at all, his tone terse. 'For the next few days you are all under *my* protection and you'll damn well do as you're told, woman. Why can't you be more like Leonora? She doesn't argue and fight over the simplest thing.'

Much as Kay loved her mother, she was hugely insulted. 'I hate you,' she said hotly, wincing at the pain in her head.

'Perhaps.' He stared down at her steadily, his silver-blue gaze so piercing she shut her eyes against it. 'But hate is the sister of love.'

'Huh.' It was the most she could manage and she kept her eyes tightly shut.

'I must be mad,' he said softly, amusement warming his voice as he walked across the room to the front door, bending down and picking up a blanket he'd placed there and wrapping it round her, ignoring her protests. 'I've got not just one redhead but four of them under my roof for Christmas.'

'But the others don't argue and fight over the simplest thing,' she reminded him bitterly, still furious.

'True.'

And he actually had the gall to chuckle as he stepped out into the icy afternoon, hooking the door shut behind him before striding down the path to the handsome vehicle waiting at the roadside, Henry at the wheel and her mother and the girls staring anxiously out of the windows, wrapped up like Eskimos.

Over the next couple of days Kay slept most of the time away, her mind more at rest when Emily threw off the worst of the bug overnight.

Mitchell insisted on calling in his own doctor to examine the houseful of patients, but he merely confirmed what had already been said and repeated the advice of rest, hot lemon and paracetamol.

Late Christmas Eve afternoon it started to snow, and for the first time since the flu had manifested itself Kay found she could lie and gaze out of the window without feeling as though her brain were going to break into pieces. She could hear sounds from downstairs; they had permeated her dreams once or twice over the last twenty-four hours, but she hadn't been able to make herself respond. Now her lips twitched as she heard the unmistakable sound of children's laughter. The girls were all right, thank goodness. And Henry had said her mother was feeling a little better when he'd brought her some soup earlier.

She couldn't miss being with the girls Christmas Eve. Kay forced herself to sit up, although it had been very pleasant lying in the warm cocoon with the aches and pains that had racked her body beginning to subside a little, and the big fat flakes of snow drifting past the window.

The room was luxurious—all the bedrooms were—the colour scheme one of soft golds and cream, and the carpet ankle-deep. Kay knew the twins' room was to the right of hers and her mother's on the left, but, apart from several very brief visits from Georgia and Emily, she had seen nothing of them. Henry had kept up a steady supply of light nourishing 'invalid' food, and Mitchell had made the odd appearance, but she had felt too out of it to do more than open her eyes for a few minutes at a time.

Kay flung back the duvet and swung her legs over the side of the bed, making her way slowly to the bathroom. It was a great effort and she had to rest several times before her toilette was finished, but eventually she was washed and dressed, her hair free of tangles and tied back from her face. She sat on the bed for a few minutes after she was ready, amazed at how tired she felt. In the past she'd had the occasional heavy cold and labelled it the flu. She now made a mental note never to do that again. The real thing was so different.

Once she was on the landing she could hear children's laughter and followed the sound. She noticed the staircase had been decorated with fresh garlands of holly and ivy and there were more in the hall once she reached the bottom of the stairs, but it was as she pushed open the drawing-room door and stood quietly surveying the scene within that she had her biggest surprise.

The room had been transformed into a glittering festive pageant, tinsel and ornamentation decorating the walls and every available surface or so it seemed to Kay's dazed eyes, but it was the eight-foot Christmas tree that really drew the eye. It stood in regal splendour at the far end of the room, its branches bedecked with glittering trinkets, baubles and tinsel and the huge tub that held it surrounded with gaily wrapped parcels.

Emily was lying on one of the sofas, which had been pulled close to the blazing fire, busily threading a paper chain with Henry, her mother was lying on another sofa close by in her dressing gown with a blanket over her legs, and Mitchell and Georgia were sitting together on the floor wrapping a parcel.

It was a charming scene, a homely and comfortable one, which suggested the five of them were totally at ease in each other's company, and as Kay watched she felt suddenly cold. She was the one on the outside looking in. Ridiculous, maybe, but that was how she felt.

And then Emily looked up and saw her, her shriek of delight causing the others to glance towards the door. Within a moment Georgia was at Kay's side, taking her hand and leading her over to sit beside Emily—Henry having moved—as both little girls began talking nineteen to the dozen.

'Do you like the Christmas tree and everything, Mummy? We did it as a surprise for you.'

'And there are presents for you and Grandma under the tree but we're not allowed to say what they are.'

'Ours are with Father Christmas. Uncle Mitch has written to tell him we're here for Christmas so he can bring our sacks here.'

'It's taken us ages to get everything nice, Mummy.'

This last from Georgia was a little uncertain. Kay realised her face must be betraying her, but the 'Uncle Mitch' had hit her like a savage punch in the solar plexus. This was exactly what she'd feared, the reason she'd made it a policy not to date while the children were small, why she'd hesitated particularly with regards to Mitchell Grey. She didn't want her girls to be made conversant with 'uncles'. She knew friends in a similar situation to herself and no sooner had their children got used to one uncle than he disappeared and another took his place. Uncles were transient. It stood to reason, didn't it, that if the fathers of the children weren't prepared to stick around, uncles were going to be even less reliable? And Mitchell had already laid out the ground rules well in advance.

She had been foolish to think she could keep the two lives separate—that of having a light 'friendship' with Mitchell, and that of her real life with her babies. But it would have been all right, it would, if she hadn't got sick.

She forced a bright smile to her face as she pulled Emily onto her lap, and put an arm round Georgia, who was standing at her knee. *Pretend; don't spoil their Christmas.* 'It's absolutely beautiful, my darlings. You must have been so busy. I can't believe it.'

Her gushing must have worked because both children's faces became animated again, their chattering washing over her as she met Mitchell's eyes. They were narrowed on her face, the ice-blue depths glinting as though he had read her mind.

She stared at him, knowing she ought to say something but her mind registering only the dark attractiveness at the root of his maleness. He was in a light shirt and jeans, his feet bare, and his hair looked ruffled. She had never seen it like that before. Usually it was ruthlessly sleek and impeccable, like him. This was another Mitchell; she was seeing yet one more facet of his complex persona and, if anything, although this being was more casual and laid-back than any so far, it disturbed her the most. It was the most human, seemingly the most approachable, and it was an illusion.

'Darling, how are you feeling?' Her mother's voice from the sofa some feet away brought Kay's head turning. 'We looked in on you an hour or so ago when I came down, but you were fast asleep.'

Kay forced another smile as she said, 'A bit shaky but much better.'

'This is my first time up too.' Whether Leonora had guessed how she'd felt when she had watched them all from the doorway, Kay didn't know, but her mother continued, 'Not that you could really call it that when I was all but carried down here and then tucked up and forbidden to move. All this work has been done over the last day, apparently.'

'The girls needed something to take their minds off missing their mother,' Mitchell said softly, speaking to Leonora but with his eyes on Kay's pale face.

Kay nerved herself to meet his gaze again. 'You've been very kind to us, thank you,' she said stiffly. 'I can't believe all the trouble we've put you to.'

'No trouble.' He had risen to his feet when Georgia had rushed to meet her, his hands thrust in his pockets and his dark face inscrutable. 'That's what friends are for, after all.'

Colour flooded into her pale face. He *had* sensed her thoughts earlier.

'Besides which, it's given Henry and myself the chance to act like boys again, eh, Henry?' His voice was mocking. 'We might even be persuaded to build a snowman if the snow falls thickly enough over Christmas.'

'I've never made a snowman.' Georgia had left Kay's

side before she could stop her, walking across and tugging on Mitchell's jean-clad leg to get his attention. 'There was only a teeny weeny bit of snow last year and it melted.'

'It did? That's a shame, munchkin.' Mitchell put out a hand and ruffled the child's curls. 'I tell you what, I'll put in an order with Father Christmas to leave enough snow for a snowman this year. How about that? Then we can make one with big coal eyes and a carrot nose.'

'Emily can't go out into the cold.' Georgia looked artlessly up at her hero. 'She'll have to stay inside and watch.'

'No, I won't.' Emily's lower lip began to tremble. 'I want to build a snowman too.'

Four years old and they were fighting over him already, Kay thought helplessly. What was it about Mitchell Grey and the female race? Even her mother had a glow about her that wasn't due to the heat from the huge coal fire burning in the hearth.

'Emily will be fine all wrapped up in a day or two,' Mitchell said firmly, his tweak of Georgia's nose letting the tot know he wasn't falling for it. 'Building a snowman is a job for everyone to do together or not at all. Okay?'

Georgia nodded adoringly and Kay groaned silently. He had her feisty little Georgia eating out of the palm of his hand. They were going to hear nothing but 'Uncle Mitchell' for months after this.

'Now, there just happens to be two early Christmas presents for two little girls I know on the Christmas tree.' Mitchell grinned at the twins. 'See if you can find them. Not under the tree, mind. On it.'

Emily was off Kay's lap and across to the tree only seconds after her sister, and they found the parcels without any trouble. On opening, the boxes revealed two beautifully dressed, long-haired dolls, complete with muffs and capes and other accessories, identical but for the fact one doll was dressed in silver and the other in gold.

Kay watched as the girls came dancing back to thank Mitchell without any prompting, and when he said the dolls were from both himself and Henry they immediately went to Henry and hugged him too, before settling down on the rug in front of the fire and beginning to play with their new babies.

'They're two lovely little girls, Kay. You're bringing them up very well.'

Henry was sitting with her mother now and as Mitchell joined her on the sofa Kay felt herself tense. 'Thank you.'

'How are you feeling?' he asked softly.

He was sitting close but not too close. Nevertheless every nerve in her body had twanged and now she found herself utterly unable to break the hold of his eyes. 'I...I'm surprised how weak I feel.' She hadn't meant to be so honest but the nearness of him had totally thrown her.

'You haven't eaten anything but mush for twenty-four hours,' he said just as softly, his delineation of Henry's superb homemade soups and soufflés grossly unfair, 'besides which the news has been full of how this particular strain of influenza has young and old and everyone between off their feet. It's nasty.'

'Georgia still seems okay.' She glanced towards the girls, their curls like living flames in the glow of the fire. 'Right from a tiny baby, bugs just seem to bounce off her somehow, whereas poor Emily catches everything that's going.'

'It must have been tough being sole parent, especially when they were first born.'

Her hands twisted in her lap. 'Sometimes.' She kept her eyes on the two small heads. 'But they more than made up for any difficulties,' she said defensively, 'and they've always been very happy children. They haven't wanted for anything.'

'I wasn't criticising,' he said soothingly, 'and I can see what a great mother you've been and are.'

'Perry would have been a terrible father. He only ever thought of himself and would have made their lives miserable. The fact that he has never even tried to see them proves that.'

'Kay, for what it's worth I think you did the only thing you could when you threw him out.' He stared at her. 'Were there people who said you should have stayed with him regardless?' he asked quietly. 'For the sake of the children?'

'A few.' And it had hurt, terribly, even though she'd told herself they had no idea what had gone on behind closed doors.

Anger thickened his voice. 'Fools are always the first to give an opinion. I was brought up in a home that resembled a war zone for a great deal of the time. Believe me, the twins are very fortunate. You have two normal, well-adjusted and happy little girls; they're a testimony to the fact that you were right in the course of action you followed. Don't ever doubt that, not for a minute.'

Funny, but she hadn't expected such understanding and comfort from him, not from Mitchell. She hadn't spoken of how she felt to a living soul before this, not even her mother, but he had seemed instinctively to guess the doubts and fears she managed to keep under lock and key most of the time. With her father having died when he did, the girls had never really had a male figure in their lives, apart from her brother, and Peter was too busy with his own family to spend much time with them.

'Better no father at all than one who would have put them through hell, Kay.'

He took her hand, feeling it flutter in his before it became still.

The sky was dark outside the warmth of the house, but with the snow steadily falling a winter wonderland was forming in the garden, its glow luminescent in the light from the windows. Her mother and Henry were still talking quietly together, their voices too low to be overheard, and the twins were busy with their dolls, and it just seemed the moment to say, 'It's affected you deeply, the way your father was, hasn't it.'

She saw his jaw clench and for a moment she thought he was going to draw away. Instead his hand tightened on hers. 'It was my mother who was a serial adulteress.' It was bald and flat. 'It got in the end so it was any man, any time, but long before that I knew she didn't love my father or my sister and I. I don't think she was capable of love in any form.'

'You...you knew she was having affairs, even though you were just a boy?' Kay whispered.

'I can't remember a time I didn't know,' he said bitterly. 'They would row—no, that's too mild a word for what went on. They would fight, quite literally, at times. She'd fly at him and he'd try and hold her off for a while, but she always pushed him too far. She broke his arm once; I was about nine at the time and I can remember his scream when she brought a poker down on him. He said he was leaving then, but of course he didn't. Don't ask me why because I don't think he loved her any more.'

'Oh, Mitchell.' Pain streaked through her. Pain for him now, and for the small, bewildered little boy he had once been. For the sister who had also been embroiled in the madness. 'Your sister? Was she younger than you?'

He nodded. 'I used to look after her as much as I could; she was a sweet kid, timid. Scared to death of our mother.

Most times when we'd get home from school the house would be empty. Dad would get home from work, sometimes before she got back and other times after. She never tried to deny where she had been or with whom. She was very honest.' His mouth twisted bitterly.

'I got a couple of paper rounds, one before school and one after. I think I'd got some crazy idea of saving enough to take Kathleen, my sister, and I away somewhere. Normally I was back long before Dad got in but this particular night my bike got a puncture. From what the neighbours said, Dad was waiting for my mother when she got home and when he found out she was seeing a man he worked with, he dragged her to the car to go and confront him at his home in front of his wife and family. Why he took Kathleen with him I don't know—perhaps it was to make this guy feel bad, or because he didn't want to leave her alone in the house. There was a head-on collision with a lorry anyway. End of story.'

Kay put her other hand on top of his, pressing it as she said, 'It wasn't your fault, Mitchell. You weren't to know he would do that, that he'd take Kathleen with him.'

He shrugged powerful shoulders. 'I was all Kathleen had; she trusted me. I should have been there. I wouldn't have let her go with them.' His voice was so raw she blinked against it.

'Perhaps your father would have made you go too and you'd all have been killed. Four lives lost instead of three.'

'For a long time I wished it had been that way.' He looked her full in the face, his mouth twisting. 'I was an angry young man, Kay. Very angry, very bitter, very foolhardy. I did some things I'm not proud of and it was more by luck than judgement I didn't end up in prison. Then one day a group of us were racing each other on motorbikes. One of my friends was killed in front of my eyes. It brought me up short. I realised I wanted to live after all.'

'I'm glad you did,' she said softly. She hadn't meant to say it the way it had sounded. Her voice hadn't been nearly as matter-of-fact or prosaic enough. But what really scared her half to death was the consuming urge to comfort him, to take the look of bleakness out of his eyes and to kiss the hard set of his mouth until it relaxed beneath her lips. Friends. The word mocked her. The feelings she had for Mitchell were not ones of friendship, they never had been, and they didn't remotely resemble the starry-eyed infatuation and girlish love that had led her to marry Perry either.

A CD of Christmas carols had been playing in the background and now, as it finished, Mitchell rose to his feet. 'There's a cartoon called *Santa's Special Christmas* starting about now. Fancy watching it, girls?' he asked Georgia and Emily.

Kay stared at him as he walked across to the huge television set and switched it on. Was it her imagination— part of the shock of acknowledging how she felt about him—or had his action been a deliberate withdrawal? Did he feel he'd said too much, revealed too much? How did she handle this?

As the twins positioned themselves at a suitable distance in front of the TV clutching their dolls, Kay lay back against the sofa and shut her eyes. She was aware of Mitchell walking across the room again but when she opened her eyes she saw he had picked up the blanket that had been wrapped round Emily, and was now tucking it round the small child as she sat with Georgia on the floor. The action was so poignant for some reason that Kay wanted to cry.

'Do you think you ladies could manage a sherry now you're in the land of the living again?' Mitchell included Leonora in the smile he gave, and when Kay and her mother both accepted and Henry made a move to rise he waved the older man down, saying, 'Stay where you are, Henry, I'll get them. A drop of your usual?'

Kay had to admit she thoroughly enjoyed the rest of the evening, even though she dozed off twice before dinner.

Georgia and Emily were so excited it was no use insisting on their normal bedtime, and so the little girls ate dinner at the elaborately festive dining table with the grown-ups, beside themselves with delight. They were almost asleep over their dessert, and when Mitchell picked them up, one on each arm, Kay went with him to tuck her daughters into bed. She was aware it was all too cosy, too intimate, but she couldn't do a thing about it for the time being, she told herself helplessly. It wasn't as though she had chosen to inflict them all on him, it had just...happened.

Both children were asleep as their heads touched the pillows, so worn out by all the excitement of the day and the anticipation of the morrow that they didn't need a reminder to go straight to sleep if they wanted Father Christmas to come.

Mitchell didn't hurry her to leave, standing with her as she watched the sleeping children for a couple of minutes. 'You love them very much, don't you?' he said softly.

It was on the tip of her tongue to say, Of course I do, they are my children, but, remembering all he had said downstairs, she answered simply, 'They're my world.'

Mitchell expelled a quiet breath. 'I know.' He turned his head, lifting her face up to his with one finger in the slumbering stillness as he murmured, his tone rueful, 'I thought it was going to be all so simple, dating you.'

'And it isn't?'

'No, it damn well isn't and you know it. You do know it, don't you, Kay? I want you, need you.' He drew her out of the room as he spoke, shutting the door quietly behind them and then taking her into his arms on the shadowed landing. He didn't have to tell her what he wanted, the desire was there to read in his eyes, his mouth hungry as it took hers.

Kay clung to him, her head whirling less with the after effects of the flu and more with the feel of his hard body against hers. She kissed him back; she couldn't help it. She always kissed him back—that was the effect Mitchell Grey had on her, she thought with a thread of bitterness for just a second before it was burnt up in the liquid heat coursing through her body.

His hand was in the small of her back to steady her and she gasped as the other cupped one of her breasts, his fingers beginning a languorous rhythm on its sensitive peak that had her stifling a moan of pleasure.

Something had happened, she told herself bewilderedly. There was a release of the restraint he had shown thus far. This gentle eroticism was as deliberate as it was powerful; he was forcing her to acknowledge her own need of him in the age-old way. Little did he know she'd got there before him...

His mouth and hands had complete mastery over her quivering senses, her body melting against his as he kept up the barrage of sweet sensation, fuelling her own passion with his. She thought briefly of the times Perry had made love to her, taking her with barely a kiss beforehand and thinking only of his own pleasure. What would it be like to *really* be loved by Mitchell? she asked herself dazedly. To lie with him all night, to explore and stroke and kiss every inch of that hard-muscled male body and to let him do the same to her. Because he would want to; she knew he would want to. Not for Mitchell a quick, brief coupling.

He had moved, pressing her back against the wall of the landing, and she could feel his thighs hard against hers, her softness stamped with the rock-hard power of his arousal. It was heady, intoxicating, to know how much he wanted her; it made her alive to the potency of her femininity in a way she had never experienced before.

There were sounds in the hall below them, then Henry's voice saying something to her mother as he opened the dining-room door and a faint whiff of coffee in the air. She felt Mitchell slowly draw away with a low groan of regret, his chest rising and falling with the force of his need as he straightened. 'We have to go,' he said huskily. 'Unfortunately.'

'Yes.' She was breathing hard, her cheeks flushed and her hands trembling at the tumult of desire he had released. She hadn't known she was capable of feeling like that, not in a hundred years, and now he wasn't holding her any more she felt dizzily adrift.

She raised a shaking hand to her hair, stumbling slightly, and immediately his hands came out to steady her, his voice rueful as he said, 'Damn it, I forgot you're still far from well. You've only been up five minutes and I've practically eaten you alive. Why can't I keep my hands off you?'

'I don't know.'

'I do. It's because you're enticing, mouth-watering—'

'Me?' In spite of herself Kay smiled. 'I'm not one of your gorgeous model-type females, Mitchell, as I'm only too aware. I do have mirrors in the house, you know.'

He let go of her, stepping back a pace and surveying her through eyes that were brilliantly clear in the darkness of his face. 'One, I don't have a harem of gorgeous model types, Kay,' he said quietly, his voice holding the edge of irony. 'Two, whatever you see when you look in the mirror, I see a warm and beautiful woman who is yet to be fully awakened to the power of her charm. And three, I never say anything I don't mean.'

She stared at him, her eyes locked with his, and then he moved closer again, his thumb stroking her cheek in a caressing gesture that brought a lump to her throat. 'Red hair that glows like fire when the light catches it, brown eyes as deep and soft as velvet, skin so delicate and fine it's like porcelain. How can you not see all that, Kay?'

She didn't dare believe this meant anything beyond what was for him a tried and tested seduction technique. He had *told* her he didn't want commitment or anything lasting; he had been totally up front about it. Maybe if she didn't have the twins, if she were answerable only to herself without any responsibilities, it would be different. Maybe then she would take a chance and give herself to him, hoping he would come to love her eventually, that when the time came to say goodbye he wouldn't be able to let her go.

But she did have the twins. She couldn't mess with their security or stability, neither did she have the luxury of being able to flirt with emotional suicide. And whatever he said, she still couldn't quite bring herself to believe that a man like Mitchell Grey—a man who could have any woman he wanted—would be interested in someone like her for long. She was five feet five of ordinary womanhood. She had freckles, her breasts were too small and her bottom was too big, and at that certain time of the month her skin could erupt like Mount Vesuvius. Whereas he... He was perfect.

Perry had hurt her but she had picked herself up, dusted herself down and got on with life. But if Mitchell betrayed her, if she gave herself to him and then he tired of her...

She turned her head from his intent gaze, shrugging her shoulders and making her voice as light as she could. 'Beauty is in the eye of the beholder, isn't that what they say? And hadn't we better go down now?'

'Sure.' He made no attempt to touch her. 'But it's only fair to let you know I never give up, Kay. I always get what I want.'

She felt more vulnerable than she'd ever felt in her life. Even after Perry had gone and she'd realised she had a pregnancy and then single parenthood to face, she hadn't felt such a sense of desperation, but she couldn't let him see how he had affected her. She forced herself to start walking towards the top of the stairs, tossing over her shoulder, 'Ah, but do you always get what you deserve, Mr Grey?'

She heard him chuckle. '*Touché*, Mrs Sherwood.'

This was still just a game to him. As they began to descend the stairs she felt exhaustion sweep over her in a great wave. Thank goodness she hadn't done what she'd wanted to do a few minutes ago and thrown herself into his arms, telling him she was his for as long as he wanted her. Madness. That was what he created in her: madness.

As they entered the dining room Kay saw her mother glance at her, and then Leonora said, consternation in her voice, 'Darling, you're as white as a sheet. You've done far too much on your first day up.'

'I am tired.' Kay seized the opportunity, but it was the truth anyway. She suddenly didn't know how she was going to put one foot in front of the other to climb the stairs again. 'I'm going to go to bed, if you don't mind?' She included the three of them in her swift glance. 'Goodnight, and happy Christmas.'

'I'll see you up the stairs—we don't want you falling headlong, do we?' Mitchell said silkily, ignoring her protests as he took her arm, saying to the other two, 'I'll be back in a second, and I'll have my coffee black, Henry, with a brandy.'

'I can manage perfectly well, thank you,' Kay muttered once they were at the foot of the stairs. 'Go back and have your coffee.'

'Bossy little wench, aren't you?' He grinned down at her but his eyes were thoughtful as they took in her pale face and the shadows under her eyes. 'Your mother's right, damn it, you have done too much. I shall have to watch that in the future.'

She couldn't take much more of this. For some reason she felt as though every single nerve end was exposed tonight.

'Right, let's get you into bed.' It was deliberately wicked and she opened her mouth to make a tart retort that never got voiced, Mitchell cutting it off by the simple expedient of whisking her up into his arms.

'Put me down, Mitchell. I can walk.'

'Perhaps, but this is nicer.' He looked down at her as he mounted the stairs, taking her mouth in a hard, swift kiss that took Kay's breath away.

He was too strong to fight, too powerful. She sagged against the hard wall of his chest, willing the moment to go on for ever. She wished she were a tall, stunning blonde with the sort of vital statistics to drive a man wild; she wished *he* hadn't been hurt so badly by the one woman in his life he should have been able to trust, and who had shaped the young boy Mitchell into the man he now was; she wished—oh, she wished for all sorts of things and all of them pipe dreams.

He was holding her closely, securely, as they reached the bedroom. He set her down outside the door, looking down at her quizzically as he said, 'I presume you want me to leave you here?'

No. No, she didn't. 'Yes, please. Mitchell, the girls' presents? We usually leave them in a pillowcase under the tree at home.'

'All taken care of. Henry and I have got them ready and we'll leave them there before we retire. Leonora said there's also a small matter of a glass of sherry and mince pie? We'll make sure the glass is suitably sooty and most of the mince pie's eaten, of course. Santa has to keep his strength up.'

'Thank you.'

'My pleasure,' he said softly. 'It's been fun.'

'Your home being turned upside down with a houseful of invalids?' Kay said disbelievingly.

He smiled as he lowered his head, his kiss tender and painfully sweet this time. His body was bent over her but no part was touching except his mouth fused to hers. 'You're here,' he said huskily as he straightened. 'That makes it fun.'

'Goodnight, Mitchell. Happy Christmas.' It was a whisper and she opened the door as she spoke, stepping inside the room quickly and closing the door without looking at him again. She stood leaning against the wood for several moments, however, her heart beating fast and her legs trembling.

Christmas Eve, a magical time.

Tired as she was, she levered herself off the door and

walked across to the window, looking down into the snow-covered garden for a minute or two before she drew the curtains.

But it was no good wishing for the moon.

CHAPTER SEVEN

THE twins must have been tired out with all the excitement and anticipation of Christmas Eve, because it was after seven o'clock when Kay's bedroom door was flung open and two tiny pyjama-clad little figures hurled themselves onto the bed.

'Mummy! It's Christmas morning!'

'The baby Jesus is born, Mummy.'

This last exclamation was from Emily, the ever practical Georgia adding, 'Has Father Christmas been? Has he left our presents?'

'I don't know, my darlings.' Kay had slept deeply and dreamlessly and now, as she struggled up in bed, brushing her hair out of her eyes and hugging each little wriggling girl, she added, 'Shall we go and see what's under the tree?'

'What a good idea.'

The deep male voice from the doorway brought the twins bouncing round and Kay hastily pulling the duvet up to her chin. Mitchell was leaning against the door post, his hair ruffled and his face unshaven, and Kay's heart gave a kick like a mule. He was dressed in a black silk robe and matching pyjama bottoms, and he looked more sexy than any man had the right to first thing in the morning.

'I presume Grandma will want to come and join in the proceedings?' Mitchell asked Kay, his eyebrows raised. And at her nod, added, 'Go and get her, girls, but gently, okay? Wake her gently.'

As the twins scampered past him he ruffled each head of curls and then, to Kay's horror, came further into the room, walking across to the bed. 'What do you think you're doing?' she yelped weakly.

'Saying good morning.' He bent and kissed her, hard. 'Good morning,' he said softly.

'You shouldn't be here.' She hadn't even brushed her hair or cleaned her teeth, and with the twins and her mother next door...

Mitchell raised mocking eyebrows. 'Excuse me, but I was under the impression I live here?' he said lazily, purposely misunderstanding. 'Besides, it's not the first time I've seen you in bed. You've been here three days.'

'I was ill before.'

'Don't be so school-marmish,' he reproved her sternly.

'Mitchell, *please*.'

'I'm going to have to work on those inhibitions of yours.' He gave her one last swift kiss on the tip of her nose and walked over to the door, saying, 'You were more fun when you were ill, tossing and turning quite deliciously at times, I might add. Are you wearing that nightie with the very thin straps that's almost transparent?'

'You...you peeping Tom!' She was blushing crimson and furious with herself for doing so.

'Could I help it if you kept throwing off your covers in gay abandon?' he protested innocently.

'You, you...'

'Get your dressing gown on and make yourself decent, woman. There's children around.'

He grinned at her and she glared at him.

'Tut-tut.' He shook his head sorrowfully. 'Where's your Christmas spirit, Kay? Goodwill to all men and so on.' He shut the door on her splutterings but not before he added, 'And you'd better be quick; Georgia and Emily are raring to go.'

They all went down together in the end, even Henry joining them on the landing and looking very distinguished in a pair of dark aubergine cotton pyjamas and a striped dressing gown.

Once the twins had indulged in an orgy of unwrapping, delving into their pillowcases until they were empty, Mitchell nodded to Henry and the older man left the room briefly to return with the most enormous brightly wrapped package.

'This is from Henry and myself, girls,' Mitchell said softly. 'Happy Christmas.'

It was a doll's house, complete with beautifully fashioned furniture and a little family of dolls right down to a baby in a crib. The twins were ecstatic.

The adults then exchanged gifts, and Kay was thankful she had bought something for Mitchell, and a little present for Henry, before she'd fallen ill. However, the leather driving gloves and cashmere scarf that Mitchell seemed to receive with genuine pleasure paled into insignificance beside the dainty white-gold and diamond watch he presented her with.

'Oh, Mitchell, it's beautiful.' As he fastened it on her wrist she stared down in wonder. She had never thought to own anything so exquisite, but it must have cost a *fortune*. And gloves and a scarf... 'But I didn't get you anything nearly so nice.'

He shushed her by putting a finger on her lips. 'I needed new gloves and the scarf is perfect,' he said softly. 'You needed a new watch. I noticed your present one was always stopping or told the wrong time.'

Kay thought it was very nice of him not to mention at this point that her old one also had the gilt flaking off. It had been a quick buy off a market stall the year before but all she could afford at the time, the twins just having needed new shoes and a winter coat each. She looked at him, her eyes enormous. 'Thank you,' she said trem-blingly, wondering why—after such a marvellous gift—she should want to cry.

'Tea, toast and croissants everyone?' Henry cut across the moment, suddenly reverting to housekeeper and cook. 'I'm not going to cook a full English breakfast because I want you to do justice to Christmas dinner, which will be served promptly at one o'clock. And woe betide anyone who says they're not hungry. No excuses about post-flu appetites either,' he added warningly.

'Can I come and help you?'

This was from Leonora, and when Henry said, 'That would be most welcome, thank you,' in his old-fashioned way, Kay caught Mitchell staring at his friend in open astonishment.

'What is it?' she whispered when the other two had disappeared in the direction of the kitchen, and only the girls remained, playing contentedly with the doll's house. 'Why did you look at Henry like that?'

Mitchell smiled, a curiously satisfied smile. 'Because in all my years of knowing Henry he's never allowed anyone to storm the bastion of his kitchen,' he said thoughtfully, 'and I mean no one, full stop.'

Kay stared at him as the import of his words dawned. 'You don't mean...'

'I think Henry rather likes your mother.' He watched her for a minute, seeing her absorb the idea. 'Would you mind?' he asked quietly.

Would she? It might make things a little difficult when she and Mitchell stopped seeing each other, but if her mother liked Henry and the feeling was reciprocated, that was wonderful. If nothing else it would give her mother an interest beyond that of her own family. 'No,' she said firmly. 'I wouldn't mind at all.'

It started to snow again as they were having breakfast, but when Kay said she wanted Emily to wait another day before she went outside to build the snowman the twins didn't object too much, content to play with all their new toys. Hence the morning was a lazy one of sitting by the roaring fire watching the children play while they listened to carols on the radio, the four adults talking of this and that as the smell of roasting turkey began to permeate the air.

After Henry served particularly wicked elevenses of coffee laced with Tia Maria and spices and topped with whipped cream, along with a plateful of his delicious home-made shortbread, Kay settled back on the sofa next to Mitchell in a haze of festive well being. She awoke some time later with the embarrassing realisation that she must have dozed off, her head now lodged comfortably on his chest and his arm holding her close as she curled into him.

She stiffened, raising her head cautiously only to stare into a pair of bright blue eyes. 'You don't snore when you're asleep,' he said conversationally, 'but you do make the most enchanting little sniffles now and again, like a small animal making itself more cosy.'

Kay could feel heat flooding her cheeks and now Mitchell laughed softly, straightening as he said, 'You're not the only one who had a nap. Look over there.' She looked and saw her mother was dead to the world too, stretched out on another sofa with a blanket over her lower half. 'It'll do you both good; you still look peaky.'

Peaky? What did that mean? A mess? Something the

cat wouldn't deign to drag in? 'Where are the girls?' she asked, more to change the subject than anything else.

'Helping Henry make a batch of muffins for tea. Apparently he was brought up with muffins for tea on Christmas Day afternoon, and as this Christmas seems to have turned into a family affair...' He shrugged.

Did he mind? There had been an inflexion in his voice Kay couldn't quite fathom. He must have had other plans for Christmas after all. A man like Mitchell Grey didn't sit at home twiddling his thumbs.

He had bent to nuzzle her curls with his chin, murmuring almost to himself, 'You smell wonderful. What is it you're wearing?'

'Baby powder.'

'Baby powder?' He leaned back to stare at her. 'You're joking.'

She shook her head. 'When you carried me off I wasn't in a fit state to think of perfume or cosmetics,' she reminded him. 'The twins had some baby lotion and powder in their toiletries so I'm using that.'

He shook his head, his eyes bright with laughter. 'Do you mean to tell me that I've spent a fortune over the years on expensive perfume as gifts, and all the time I could have got away with baby powder?'

She stared at him. It was unintentional—probably—but suddenly she was reminded yet again that he was a 'love 'em and leave 'em' type. She breathed deeply. 'I don't think the sort of women you date would appreciate baby powder, Mitchell,' she said evenly. 'Do you? I'm a mother; that smell has been second nature to me for years.'

He wasn't smiling any longer. 'Meaning?'

'Meaning nothing,' she said carefully, 'except that they're used to Chanel and Gucci, and I'm used to baby powder and off the peg, that's all. They could be ready to fly off round the world or attend an elegant function at the drop of the hat; I have to make sure my mother can babysit and even then half my mind is on the girls if one of them is poorly or upset about something. Two very different worlds.'

They both knew what she was saying. 'Unbridgeable?' he asked softly.

No, not unbridgeable. In fact if there was even the prospect he could offer something beyond a brief affair, she would build the bridge herself, brick by brick. She gave a brittle smile. 'I think so. It's a case of butterflies and moths, I suppose.'

'You're not a moth,' he said roughly, a hardness entering his tone. 'Not unless you choose to be.'

'My option to choose ended four years ago.' She eyed him bravely, inwardly shaking and outwardly composed. 'And I wouldn't have it any other way. All the Chanel and Gucci in the world couldn't begin to compare with my children's smiles. Cartier diamonds are nothing compared to a gaudy plastic ring and bracelet I have at home, things they got from some crackers that they think are wonderful but which they gave to me.'

He nodded. 'I can buy that.'

'But you can't buy it, don't you see? They give me their unconditional love and trust and I have to do everything I can to make sure their world is not shaken or disturbed,' she said, deliberately misunderstanding his words. 'They're little children, Mitchell. They don't understand about moving on, and temporary liaisons, and being replaced, and I don't want them to, not yet. Time enough for all that when they're grown up and making their own way in the world. They'll probably experience rejection and loss then. For now stability and a solid foundation is what is important. They'll make lots of mistakes of their own; they're bound to. That's life. But I don't ever want them to suffer through a mistake I make, no more than they have already by not having a father.'

There was a vibrating silence for a moment. She hadn't meant to say that last bit, Kay thought distractedly; in fact she hadn't even been aware it was there, buried deep in her subconscious. But she *had* made a mistake in marrying a rat like Perry, and her babies *were* paying for it in not having a father figure.

'You can't blame yourself because Perry turned out like he did, Kay,' Mitchell said at last. 'Nothing in life comes with a cast-iron guarantee.'

Her mother was beginning to stir, and now Kay said quickly and dismissively, 'I know that.'

'Do you? I don't think so.'

She couldn't do this. She really couldn't do this. In a small voice she said, 'Can we talk about this some other time?'

He nodded, lifting her chin, which had drooped, before he murmured, 'It strikes me we've got a lot of talking to do. That wall you built to repel intruders is still steel-clad, isn't it?'

The wall *she* had built? What about the one he'd constructed? She stared at him. 'You were the one who said we're two of a kind,' she reminded him quietly. 'You've done some building work of your own, Mitchell.'

There was no time to say anything more before the twins returned, flushed and proud from their cooking efforts, and woke Leonora fully. But all through Henry's delicious Christmas lunch and the afternoon that followed Kay found herself going over what she'd said time and time again until her head was spinning. Had she said too much? Probably. Very probably, she admitted. But it was too late now.

They had muffins with the twins at five o'clock and it was obvious the two little girls were tired out even then. By six they'd had their bath and were in their pyjamas snuggled down in bed, looking impossibly angelic as Kay kissed them goodnight.

'Where's Uncle Mitchell?' Georgia asked sleepily as Kay dimmed the light. 'Isn't he going to kiss us goodnight?'

'Not tonight, darling, he's talking to Grandma and Henry.' Kay had made it clear—not so much by what she'd said as what she hadn't—that she intended to settle the children down herself without any help before she had left the drawing room. She had seen Mitchell look at her intently, his eyes searching her face, but he hadn't objected or attempted to follow her.

It had only been a few days but already Georgia and Emily were far too fond of Mitchell, Kay told herself as she walked slowly down the stairs to join the others. She had to calm things down, put an emotional brake on the proceedings. She had been so determined to prevent anything but the most fleeting of exchanges between Mitchell and her children in the last two months, and now here they all were actually living in his house! It was ironic in the extreme. But it couldn't continue. *They* couldn't continue.

The thought hit her hard and she bit her lip. He had been very kind to her, to all of them, and she appreciated it, she did really, but it didn't alter the facts. She had been crazy to start seeing him in the first place and now suddenly it had mushroomed into a giant tangle. The bottom line was he wanted her in his bed with no involvement other than a sexual one. She knew that, she had always known it, so all this was no one's fault but hers.

He had tried to seduce her in a hundred little ways, in fact just being with him was a seduction all in itself, but he hadn't lied to her. He had laid it on the line from the beginning; he'd been positively barefaced about his intentions. It wasn't comforting at all.

As she reached the drawing-room door she heard her mother laugh from within, a warm, carefree laugh that was almost a giggle. Kay stopped, her heart thumping. It had been years since she'd heard that laugh—the last time had been when her father was still alive, in fact.

In spite of her father's foolishness with money and his last disastrous run of speculating, which had resulted in her mother being left virtually destitute, Kay knew her parents had loved each other deeply. They had shared the sort of 'till death do us part' type of love she'd imagined she and Perry had got, but with her parents it had been real.

Now her mother was laughing with Henry. Kay's brow wrinkled. Did it mean...? And then she caught her racing thoughts, which had galloped ahead to picture them walking down the aisle.

For goodness' sake, she told herself sternly, her mother and Mitchell's housekeeper had only known each other for a few days; she mustn't read too much into something as unimportant as a laugh. She had been speaking the truth when she'd told Mitchell she was glad they liked each other, and if it did develop into something more she would still be glad. But only time would tell.

Nevertheless, Kay found she had to stand for a full minute composing herself before she felt able to open the door and join the others.

Why was life so complicated and up in the air? she

asked herself, stitching a bright smile on her face as she entered the warmth of the drawing room. And then she glanced across and met Mitchell's darkly brooding gaze from the other side of the room, and she had her answer,

CHAPTER EIGHT

WITH Henry and her mother present, Kay found it wasn't difficult to act a part for the rest of the evening. She managed to mention, fairly casually, that the twins had an invitation to a friend's birthday party in a day or two, so she felt it best they return home the day after Boxing Day. They were all *so* grateful for Mitchell's open-handed kindness, she emphasised carefully, but they must have inconvenienced him dreadfully, and now everyone was back on their feet it was better to get back to normal.

Mitchell had smiled an easy reply with his mouth but his features had been as flint-hard as his eyes, and she had tried to avoid meeting his gaze for the rest of the evening.

At eleven o'clock, when her mother had yawned for the hundredth time and had made noises about going to bed, Kay had leapt to join her, sticking to Leonora like glue as they said their goodnights to the men and then climbed the stairs to the bedrooms.

'Okay, what's wrong?' As they reached the landing Leonora took her daughter's arm, pulling her up short when Kay would have just said goodnight and entered her room. 'Have you two had a row or something?'

'More a something.'

'Why? When?' Leonora whispered. 'I thought we'd all been together today. When did you fit a row in?'

'I told you, we haven't rowed. It's just...' Kay didn't know how to put it but she knew with absolute certainty her mother would favour Mitchell whatever she said. 'Mitchell's not looking for any sort of ongoing relationship,' she hissed quietly, glancing back down the shadowed landing as though he were going to leap out any moment. 'And I don't want the twins confused and upset when he's not on the scene any more. They're growing too fond of him.'

'Who says he's planning not to be on the scene any more?' her mother asked, reasonably enough, Kay supposed.

'Me. Him. Oh...' Kay gazed at her mother irritably. 'He's made it clear his intentions are strictly *dis*honourable, okay? A few weeks or months or whatever of warming his sheets and having 'fun'—' she was beginning to really loathe that word '—and then bye-bye with no regrets on either side. That's how he operates. He spelled it out to me when we first started seeing each other, if you want to know.'

'And you still agreed to see him?' Leonora asked expressionlessly.

'Not exactly.' Kay bit on her lower lip. 'It wasn't like that. He just wouldn't take no for an answer and insisted we could date as friends. I said it was a mad idea, but—'

'He talked you round.'

'Yes.' Kay shrugged her shoulders helplessly.

'Are you sleeping with him?'

It wasn't like Leonora to ask personal questions of such a nature. Kay stared at her mother for a few moments before she said, 'No, I am not sleeping with him.'

'But you want to,' Leonora blithely stated.

'*Mum.*'

'It's a perfectly natural desire, Kay, and you are a grown woman of twenty-six.'

'I know how old I am, Mum.' She didn't believe this!

Leonora looked at her daughter's troubled face and her own softened as she put a hand on Kay's arm. 'Come into my room a moment, love. I want to talk to you properly.'

For a second it was on Kay's lips to refuse. She felt so battered and bruised emotionally she didn't feel like talking, and especially not on the Mitchell subject with his most ardent fan.

'Please, Kay?'

She nodded grumpily, and once inside Leonora's bedroom walked across to one of the two easy chairs positioned under the window and sat down. 'Well?' Her tone wasn't conducive to a heart-to-heart and she knew it. She just hoped her mother would take the hint.

Leonora seated herself in the other chair before she spoke, and then her voice was more matter-of-fact than persuasive when she said, 'Speaking as a third party, this is how I see it. You meet, he chases after you—' as Kay went to interrupt, Leonora held up her hand '—let me finish, Kay, please. I repeat, he chases after you, even after he discovered you have a family. He makes it clear he wants you and then, when you don't want to see him, he suggests you date as friends.' Her mother arched her eyebrow at this point. 'Kissing-cousin type of friends, I'm sure, but, nevertheless, he doesn't press his cause. Right?'

Kay nodded. She didn't need this. She really, *really* didn't need this.

'You get ill and he removes the whole lot of us to his home for Christmas, and, I might add, makes an enormous effort to give the children as good a Christmas as is possible in the circumstances. Right again?'

Her mother could be the most irritating person on

planet earth when she wanted to be. 'So, what's your point?'

'My *point* is, whatever he said to you in the beginning, I think he's a different man to the one you think he is.'

'Oh, *Mother*. For goodness' sake.' Kay shut her eyes, putting a hand to her brow. 'It's your most endearing quality, but also one that makes me want to scream at times like this, that you always insist on seeing the best in someone you like. Look, I know you mean well, but I think I know Mitchell better than you.'

'Has he told you how Henry came to be working for him?'

'Henry? No—no, he hasn't. I did ask once but he said it was Henry's story to tell,' Kay said flatly, wondering why on earth her mother had brought it up now.

'Well, Henry told me his story,' Leonora said, 'and I know he wouldn't mind me telling you.'

Kay wasn't so sure about this but with her mother in full flow there was no stopping her. Besides which, she admitted contritely, she was curious.

'Henry used to be one of the best-paid chefs in the country,' Leonora said with such pride that it made Kay wonder again how deeply her mother liked the tall, aristocratic housekeeper. 'He has worked in Italy, France, America—all over the world, in fact, and because he remained single he indulged in a lavish lifestyle: wine, women and song. Twelve years ago he was contacted by one of his old girlfriends. It appeared she'd had a child, a son. Henry's son. She'd never told him, they had only been together a few weeks and it was just one of those things that burnt out very quickly. She was wealthy in her own right and hadn't seen the need to inform him he was a father because she didn't need anything from him.'

Leonora sniffed here, one of her more eloquent sniffs, and Kay surmised her mother hadn't agreed with the girlfriend's decision.

'Only she did need something,' Leonora continued. 'Something it appeared only Henry might be able to give. The child was ill, very ill, and needed a bone-marrow transplant, but in spite of this woman and her family's wealth no matching donor had been found. Henry agreed to see if he could help and in so doing met the child, his son. He was a lovely boy apparently, eight years old and the image of his father. Henry's bone marrow matched but before they could do the operation the boy died.'

'Oh, Mum.' Kay was horrified, her mother's heart instantly putting herself and one of the twins in that position.

'It broke him, Kay.' Leonora stared at her daughter and they both had tears in their eyes. 'He came back to England from America where the boy had been and resumed his life, but he felt it was like his spring had snapped. He started to drink, had days off work, generally fell apart. He lost his job; got another and then lost that, and then the word went out and he was unemployable. His so-called friends didn't want to know. He'd got as low as he could go, when Mitchell saw him one day and recognised him as a chef he'd once known. Mitchell picked him up out of the gutter—literally—and took him home.'

Kay was sitting forward in her seat now, hardly breathing, transfixed as she was by the unfolding drama.

'Henry said Mitchell gave him shelter, clothes, food, but most of all friendship, even when he was at his worst. Mitchell's doctor diagnosed a breakdown and the recovery was slow, but one day Henry found he wanted to live instead of wanting to die.'

'Like Mitchell,' Kay breathed softly. And then, as her mother raised questioning eyebrows, she said, 'It doesn't matter. Go on.'

'There's not much more to tell. Henry didn't want to go back to his old life—even if he could have found places to hire him, which he probably could have done with Mitchell backing him—and as his recovery coincided with the purchase of this place Mitchell offered him a home and a job for as long as he wanted to stay.'

'You've fallen for Henry, haven't you?' Kay said gently.

Leonora blushed, an answer in itself. 'He's a good man at heart, Kay. Like Mitchell.'

They were back to Mitchell again. Kay sat back in her seat, trying to assess what was nagging at her now Henry's heartbreaking story had come to a conclusion. And then it dawned on her.

'I'm not denying he has the capacity to be amazingly kind on occasions,' she said very slowly, trying to formulate her thoughts as she spoke. 'Like he was with Henry, and with us this Christmas. But don't you see? The fact that he was so good to Henry negates your argument that I'm in some way special to him, different to the rest, and that was what you were trying to say, wasn't it?'

'Kay—'

'No, it's my turn now,' Kay said firmly. 'What he did for Henry was great, it really was, and for all we know he might have done a million and one good Samaritan deeds in his time, but that still doesn't change the way he looks at women and commitment. There are things in his past that have shaped him, things that happened when he was a boy, and it would take someone very special to help him get rid of his hang-ups. I'm—'

'Lovely,' Leonora put in quickly.

'Ordinary,' Kay said, smiling faintly. 'Face it, Mum. I am.'

'You care about him, though.'

If her mother's voice hadn't been so sad Kay might have been able to bluff her way out of it. As it was she swallowed hard, tears pricking at the back of her eyes as she fiercely told herself she couldn't cry. 'Then that's my misfortune, isn't it? I walked into this with my eyes open and I suppose I was hoping...'

'Hoping?' Leonora prompted gently.

'Hoping he might fall madly in love with me, like I have with him, the more time we've spent together over the last couple of months. Stupid.'

'Not stupid, just human.' They sat together in silence for a few moments, Leonora taking Kay's cold hands in her own warm ones. 'What will you do?'

Kay didn't answer for a little while, and then she roused herself, straightening her shoulders. 'End it. Not in a big, dramatic way because, Mitchell being Mitchell, he'll look on that as a challenge. I think that's why he was interested in the first place, because I didn't fall at his feet and worship like most women. I was different, that's all it was,' she added with a shred of bitterness. 'No, I'll do it carefully. Cut down on the dates I can keep, put up obstacles, that kind of thing.'

'And you think that will work?' Leonora asked doubtfully.

'Eventually. He's a proud man, Mum.'

They talked for a few more minutes and then Kay kissed her mother, hugging her tight for a moment before she left. Once outside on the landing she stood listening but she could hear nothing from downstairs. She walked along to the twins' room, opening the door very quietly and tiptoeing across to the little girls asleep in their beds. She stood there for some time and it wasn't until she felt the salt at the edges of her mouth that she realised she was crying. After rubbing her eyes with the back of her hand she tucked the duvets more securely around the two tiny figures, positioning their teddy bears under their arms, before leaving as silently as she had come.

On opening the door to her room Kay nearly jumped out of her skin, smothering her yelp of alarm with the palm of her hand as she realised the big dark figure sitting in one of the easy chairs was Mitchell. 'Where was the party?' he asked sarcastically, not moving a muscle as she closed the door before taking one or two steps into the room.

'I'm sorry?'

'You've been—' he consulted the Rolex on his tanned wrist '—thirty-five minutes, and this from a woman who was allegedly so tired she couldn't keep her eyes open downstairs.'

The shock of seeing him sitting there had died and healthy anger was taking its place. 'I *was* tired,' she said shortly, 'but I had a chat with my mother. That isn't a crime, is it? I looked in on the twins too,' she added crisply. 'That's what I do, Mitchell. I'm a mother.'

'So you reminded me today—exhaustively.' The crystal eyes in the handsome face were cold. 'Which brings me on to why I'm here.'

'Which you shouldn't be.' She glared at him. 'It's twenty to twelve. I'm tired.'

'Tough.' He spoke with a softness that carried true menace.

'Charming,' Kay said sharply. 'Very host-like.'

'And you needn't take that tone. You've frozen me out all this afternoon and evening and I want to know why. Is it still this "two different worlds" thing? Because if it is that's bull. Half the world's population wouldn't be with their partner right now if their past and present had to match perfectly, and you know it.'

'It's not a question of being the same in that sense, of course it's not,' she snapped hotly, the tension of the afternoon and the emotionally wearing chat with her mother stretching her nerves to breaking-point.

'Then what?' He levered himself up from the chair and Kay forced herself not to move or react as he walked across to her, her eyes wide and steady as she met his angry gaze. 'What is it? All this talk of you being a mother? Damn it, Kay, you've been a mother since I met you; Georgia and Emily haven't suddenly arrived on the scene. You must know I wouldn't ask you to upset them in any way, disrupt their routine or security. Don't make me out to be some sort of self-centred, mercenary dictator because I don't like it.'

'I didn't say you were a monster,' she fired back quickly, her heart thumping.

'Well, that's the way you've made me feel all afternoon.' He raked a hand through his short hair, the gesture one of extreme frustration and fury. 'Damn it, I've trodden on eggshells with you for the last couple of months. I've had so many cold showers it's not true, cautioned myself to go slowly until I'm half out of my mind, and for what? To be looked at as thought you're scared stiff of me one minute or that I'm something that's just crawled out of the slime the next.'

'That is so unfair! Hugely unfair.'

'No, it is not, Kay.' He was standing so close she could see where he'd nicked himself shaving, the warm, faintly delicious smell of him teasing her nostrils.

'Well, if you feel like that why have you bothered?' she said feverishly. 'Us dating was your idea, if you remember.'

'Oh, I remember, all right,' he said with more than a touch of sarcasm. 'I remember everything about that first lunch with you, believe me. It will be engrained on my memory till my dying day.' He pulled her towards him suddenly, wrapping his arms round her as if to bind her to him. 'A defiant scrap of nothing with flashing eyes and a skirt so short I was rock-hard for a week just thinking about it.' He shook her slightly, his voice holding a faint note of self-derision. 'I knew when they came and told me you'd flown the coop I should cut my losses. I didn't need aggravation in the form of a red-haired siren who was intent on telling me to go to blazes. But you'd got under my skin, even then.'

She stared up at him, unable to say a word. His eyes were very silvery in the light of the one bedside lamp he had clicked on, the blue almost non-existent. She knew what was happening; the dark magnetism that was at the heart of his charm had reached out yet again to convince her black was white and white was black. She *knew* the sensible thing would be to end this right now, but standing here locked in his arms, with his anger dying and being replaced by something very different, logic and reason went out of the window.

But she had to try. She tensed, pulling back a little.

'This is crazy,' she whispered. 'It can't work, you must see that. We're too different, Mitchell.'

'I'm getting too close. That's the real problem, isn't it?' he said softly.

She took a deep breath. 'Yes,' she said bravely, 'in a way. It...it wasn't part of the deal that you'd get to know my family. And I am grateful, really,' she rushed on, 'for all you've done, but...'

Anything else she might have said was swallowed up as his mouth descended on hers, his kiss fierce and hungry. Kay found herself clinging to him with desperate urgency, pressing closer into the hard male body as he kissed her with a raging passion that sent the blood rushing through her veins more warmly than the hot mulled wine they'd had earlier.

The thought came that she had to stop this, that it went against everything she had been thinking and talking about, but she couldn't bear to move away. She wanted him, she needed him, and if it had to finish soon, so be it, but she could have this one night in his arms, couldn't she?

She felt weightless and light-headed, enchanted and quivering with the sensations spiralling through her body. She was barely aware he had moved them over to the bed, but then she was lying down on the soft covers and he was bent over her, his hands and his mouth creating a yearning she felt she'd die from if it wasn't properly assuaged.

'You're so beautiful, Kay. Far more beautiful than you realise, my darling.' He was kissing her eyelids, her cheeks, her lips, her throat, his mouth moving over the delicate freckled skin at the swell of her breasts and then lower. She was lost in whirling desire, the ache in her body needing his to appease it.

She hadn't felt her blouse being undone, and even when his mouth and touch registered on bare skin the sensation was too sweet to stop. Right from when she'd met him her nights had been invaded by torturous longings and wild dreams, too erotic to dwell on in the cold light of day. But now her imaginings were coming true and he was everything she'd known he would be, knowing exactly where to touch, to kiss...

Why hadn't she known it was possible to feel like this, that the mediocre sex life she had experienced with Perry wasn't the real thing? She had read in novels about a woman's body becoming a warm, pulsating, mindless energy but she had thought that it was fiction, clever writing to titillate. But this wasn't fiction, this was real.

He was stroking the silky skin of her abdomen and as her hands clasped him to her, her fingers moving under his shirt and finding the hard range of planes and muscles beneath, he groaned softly. She could feel the hard pulse of his desire and it created such a fierce excitement she didn't recognise herself.

She opened drugged eyes to see him bending over her, his face harsh and dark with passion and different from the Mitchell she knew. There was no trace of the cool, controlled entrepreneur or wry, mordacious man about town now. He wanted her, badly. She reached out to fumble with the belt in his jeans, desire making her all fingers and thumbs, and it came as a drenching shock when his hands moved over hers, stilling them.

'No, Kay.'

'No?' It was the barest of whispers, all she could manage.

He groaned, the sound wrenched from the depths of him. 'Don't look like that,' he growled huskily. 'Don't you think I want to? Hell, I'm going insane and it gets worse every time we're together, but I don't want it to be like this. That bozo you were married to; I only had to touch you once to know he had never awakened you. You responded to me like a virgin, unsure, overwhelmed by your feelings—'

'Mitchell, I have two children.' She had gone white then scarlet before hauling herself into a sitting position on the bed, desperately aware of the state of her clothing and feeling more humiliated than she'd ever felt in her life. She had thrown herself at him and he had refused her. It was the one refrain beating in her head. 'I'm no virgin.'

'Not physically maybe.' He watched her as she groped with the buttons of her blouse, her frantic haste adding to her clumsiness. 'Kay, when we make love—and we will—it will be a decision of your mind and not just your body. You will know exactly what you are doing.'

'How civilised,' she said with an attempt at derision that didn't come off at all.

'If you want to put it like that.' His voice was cold now, contained. 'Whatever, you won't have any regrets because you were swept away by emotion or curiosity or anything else. It will be your first time—in everything that counts it *will* be your first time,' he added as Kay went to protest again, 'and you will make a conscious decision as a grown woman to let me love you.'

Kay's eyes jerked to meet his at the last words. If only, *if only* he had meant that in the real sense of the word. But he was talking about sex, not love. 'And if I don't?'

she said shortly, forcing iron into her voice to combat the trembling she was trying to hide.

'You will.' It was supremely confident, and for a moment she actually hated him. 'You will come to me of your own volition and I will make you into the woman you were always meant to be. It's fate, kismet.'

'It's wishful thinking.' She didn't know where she was finding the strength to act as though her heart hadn't been just torn out by the roots, but she was grateful for it.

'Still fighting,' he said softly.

His eyes had gone to her hair and now Kay snapped, her fragile cool deserting her. 'Don't you dare mention the colour of my hair or, so help me, I'll hit you. And could you please leave my room? I was brought up to think that when one was a guest in someone's home it didn't automatically mean the host had visiting rights.'

He ignored the slur but she had seen his eyes narrow momentarily and knew he hadn't liked it. It was a poor comfort in view of all that had gone on, but better than nothing.

'Goodnight, Kay.' He walked over to the door, his tall, lean body more relaxed than it had the right to be, she thought tightly. Here was she burning up inside and knowing she would toss and turn for hours in an agony of sexual frustration, whereas he looked as cool as a cucumber. 'Dream of me.'

She glared at him. 'A very remote possibility,' she lied icily.

'"Satire should, like a polished razor keen, Wound with a touch that's scarcely felt or seen." That was written by a woman over two hundred and fifty years ago,' he said silkily. 'Do you think Lady Mary Wortley Montagu had such as you in mind?'

Kay raised her chin haughtily, two spots of bright colour still burning on her cheekbones. 'If there were men like you around, very probably.'

'Ow.' He pretended to wince as he opened the door, turning on the threshold one last time as he surveyed her, rumpled and flushed, still sitting on the bed. 'Don't forget we're building a snowman tomorrow,' he said softly. 'I want you up bright and early or else I'll have to come and fetch you.'

How *dared* he talk in that sexy, smoky voice when he had just refused her? Kay asked herself furiously. She hated him; she really *really* hated him.

She was still trying to think of an adequately scathing retort when Mitchell closed the door.

CHAPTER NINE

BOXING DAY dawned crystal-bright, the blue sky and pearly cold sunlight turning the thick snow to a carpet of shimmering white and sending the twins mad with delight.

Leonora and Henry opted for staying in the warm, so it was left to Kay and Mitchell to build the snowman with the two little girls.

The acute embarrassment Kay had felt at breakfast when she had first set eyes on Mitchell faded somewhat in the general mayhem, which involved much shrieking and rolling in the snow by Georgia, a great deal of serious and careful building by Emily and a bit of both by Mitchell, much to the delight of the twins.

When Frosty—christened so by Georgia and Emily— was finally finished, Mitchell lifted both little girls in his arms so they could put the snowman's hat and scarf in place along with his coal eyes, carrot nose and pebbled teeth.

'He's just lovely, isn't he, Mummy?' Georgia breathed reverently, turning in Mitchell's arm to hold out her hand to Kay, which immediately prompted Emily to do the same. As Kay took the mittened paws in her hands she was aware of Mitchell's eyes tight on her face, the four of them joined together in what could have been a family unit. It hurt. Unbearably.

'He's wonderful, darling,' she said brightly, her smile brittle. 'The best snowman in the world.'

Whether Mitchell had noticed the tell-tale glitter in her eyes Kay didn't know, but she felt his gaze brush over her face before he said, 'Now Frosty's all wrapped up in his hat and scarf, how about we go and feed the ducks on the lake, eh? Why don't you two go and ask Henry for some bread?'

'Can we? Really?' The twins didn't need any prompting after Kay had nodded her permission, racing off as fast as their little red wellington boots would take them.

When they had disappeared into the house there was a vibrant silence for a moment or two, and then Mitchell said softly, 'How were the dreams?'

Trust him not to pretend last night hadn't happened! The dart of anger produced enough adrenalin for Kay to be able to answer stiffly, as though he had just made a polite enquiry, 'I slept very well, thank you.'

'I didn't.' He wasn't smiling as he looked into her eyes. *Your fault.* 'Really?' She raised superior eyebrows, refusing to meet his gaze as she turned to survey the winter wonderland in front of them. 'You should try warm milk with a spot of honey. It always works for the twins.'

'I know what the cure for my disturbed sleep pattern is, Kay,' he said drily, 'and it sure as hell isn't warm milk.'

There were a hundred and one answers she could make to that, but, as she might betray herself with every one, Kay contented herself with turning her back on him and pretending to adjust Frosty's nose until Georgia and Emily reappeared two seconds later.

'Henry let us have a great big bag of bread, Mummy, and some cake too,' Georgia shouted as she hurtled towards them, Emily in her wake. 'Won't the ducks be pleased?'

The little family of ducks on Mitchell's small but charming lake were pleased, delighting the twins by coming up out of the water and taking the bread right out of the girls' fingers.

'They're virtually tame,' Mitchell said quietly, 'thanks to Henry. He went to see his sister in Kent in the spring—she keeps a smallholding, nothing grand—and while he was there a fox took the mother. He brought the eggs home still in the nest but enclosed in a polystyrene box with a hot-water bottle, so the kitchen became a duckling nursery. They all hatched and he didn't lose one of them. Would you believe the utility room off the kitchen had a paddling pool in it for weeks?'

'Really?' Kay was fascinated. She decided she thoroughly approved of Henry.

'It was a bit difficult as they grew to convince them that Henry wasn't their mother,' Mitchell said with a wry smile. 'For weeks there was the patter of tiny feet about the house if the utility-room door was left ajar. There would be Henry going to answer the door with a perfectly straight line of seven balls of fluff with webbed feet behind him.'

He grinned at her and her heart turned right over.

'Do you know that ducks have got personalities?' He turned to look at Georgia and Emily kneeling in the snow with the ducks all about them, bills opening and shutting. 'That one there in the front, the little bruiser, is called Charlie and he's the boss. And the little brown one hanging at the back is Matilda. She's the most timid one among them and yet Charlie and her are inseparable. It's like he knows she needs looking after.'

He turned to look straight at her, his gaze intensifying and the silver eyes holding hers in such a way she couldn't have spoken to save her life. Kay began to feel she were drowning in the mercurial blue orbs, which seemed to be reflecting the vivid azure of the sky; she couldn't breathe, couldn't move. There was just Mitchell in all the world.

'Have...have the others got names?' she managed at last, her voice breathless.

He smiled, a beautiful smile. 'Oh, yes.' He moved closer, taking her hand and slipping it through his arm as he pointed them out. 'That's Clarence, Lolita, Nessie, Percival and Agnes. Although Nessie might be Agnes and Agnes might be Lolita, if you get my meaning. Henry's the one who can pick them out as though they're his grandchildren.'

If she could just stand here for ever, with the blue sky above and the twins giggling and laughing as they fed Henry's little tribe, and the feel of Mitchell's hard body next to her, she would be happy. She slanted a glance at him from under her eyelashes, the big charcoal overcoat he was wearing making him even more dark and male in the white fairy-tale world surrounding them.

He must have sensed her gaze, his head turning as he looked down at her. Slowly his mouth came closer and she made no move to turn her face away. The kiss was light, sweet and warm in the frozen air and lasted no more than a breath or two, but afterwards his other hand came across hers where it rested in his arm.

'Why is it I want to lay you down in the snow and ravish you until you're moaning my name?' he asked, shockingly, a moment later, his voice a low murmur audible only to her ears.

Her eyes opened wide and she saw his mouth twist in the lopsided smile that spoke of self-derision. 'And now I've lost all the brownie points I'd gained with the account of Charlie and his tribe,' he said sadly.

She laughed, she couldn't help it, but at the same time an inner voice said despairingly, Why did he have to be so drop-dead gorgeous? She would have been satisfied with average, she really would, if Cupid could have shot his arrow into an appropriate male. But instead she had to go and fall for Mitchell. An impossible situation. An impossible man.

He kept her arm in his on the walk back to the house, the twins dancing in front of them like a pair of tiny winter sprites. Their last full day here. As they entered the house by the kitchen door Kay's heart was suddenly as heavy as lead. They would never come again; she would make sure of that. It was too sweet, too intoxicating, too dangerous. It gave her a taste of what could have been if Mitchell had felt differently.

Her mother and Henry were sitting at the kitchen table, close together, the fragrant aroma of percolating coffee scenting the air. Kay watched as Georgia and Emily ran to them, the children's faces glowing as they recounted the adventure with the ducks, and the older couple's expressions benevolent.

What would she do if this affection she could sense between her mother and Henry grew? Kay asked herself as she divested herself of her outdoor clothes. It would mean Mitchell would for ever be on the fringe of her family, even when he had someone new and she was just another of his exes. The thought stung like a scorpion.

Lunch was a cold buffet but none the less delicious for it. Henry had the enviable knack of making even the most ordinary food taste sublime, and Kay thought it showed the strength of Mitchell's will-power that he wasn't showing any signs of surplus fat on his altogether perfectly honed body.

Leonora must have had similar thoughts, because they had just finished the last of a wickedly calorie-loaded chocolate mousse when she said, 'Henry, that was wonderful but in spite of the flu I know I've put on a good few pounds. I'm amazed you and Mitchell are so slim.'

'Men are built differently to women,' Henry said factually. 'Different fat cells and so on. Besides, what does it matter?'

'Plenty when you get to my age and middle-aged spread starts showing its ugly face,' Leonora said ruefully.

'You're perfect.' Henry was looking straight into Leonora's eyes and Kay thought he'd forgotten the rest of them for a moment. 'Fat, thin, it wouldn't matter to me. *You* are perfect.'

Oh, wow! Kay glanced across at Mitchell, who raised laconic eyebrows. There was definitely something going on here all right.

Leonora had gone pink and fluttery and by unspoken mutual consent the conversation moved to safer channels, but the look in Henry's eyes and the emotion in the older man's voice stayed with Kay for the rest of the day.

It was much later, when Kay was lying in bed, that she dissected the events of the day. Building the snowman, the episode with the ducks, the way Georgia and Emily had utterly insisted Mitchell read them a story after their bath once they were tucked up in bed, the wonderful candlelit dinner Henry had cooked for the four adults and the easy laughter and camaraderie between Mitchell, Henry and her mother—it was all too beguiling. She could deceive herself very easily here—pretend it was the start of a for-ever story. But it wasn't.

'Reality check, Kay,' she whispered in the darkness. Tomorrow morning Mitchell was going to take them back to Ivy Cottage and real life would resume again. The strange cat-and-mouse game he seemed determined to play would begin once more, but this time she had to start making a few changes. Cooling things down, refusing the odd date, cutting out any contact between Mitchell and the twins so the little girls could gradually forget him. It was all for the best, it *was*, she assured herself desperately, so why did she feel she was being unfair to everyone?

She turned over onto her stomach with a sigh, angry with Mitchell, herself and the whole world.

As it happened, the return to Ivy Cottage went far easier than Kay had anticipated, mainly due to the fact that there was an emergency with Mitchell's branch in Southampton, which necessitated a personal visit from the man himself. Nevertheless, he insisted on taking Kay, her mother and the girls home even when Henry offered to do it with Kay backing the older man enthusiastically.

'Holden and his inefficient workforce can wait,' Mitchell said grimly after the call during breakfast from the manager in Southampton. 'An hour or two either way is not going to make any difference. I'm taking you back, okay?' He glared at Kay as though she had contrived the situation herself. 'And we'll call in at the supermarket on the way as planned. No argument.'

Kay nodded, said thank you and left it at that then. At least, with Mitchell having to dash off, the farewell should be brief and short-lived, no need to offer coffee or anything else that might have delayed his departure. A quick, clean and concise end to what had been a vitally disturbing and—she had to admit—wonderful Christmas.

It happened exactly as she had envisaged, and within a couple of minutes of their return to their tiny home Kay, her mother and the girls were standing waving Mitchell off from the doorstep.

'Such a shame,' Leonora murmured at the side of her as Georgia and Emily jumped up and down, waving wildly to their hero. 'It would have been nice for us to offer Henry and Mitchell a meal tonight after all they've done for us.'

Oh, no, no. She wasn't starting that. No cosy four-somes. 'We haven't got the room to entertain here, Mum.' It was firm and brooked no argument. 'Besides which, you know how I feel about things.'

Leonora pursed her lips disapprovingly. 'Darling, I wish you'd think again,' she said quietly. 'Henry is sure Mitchell is very fond of you.'

'I've no doubt he has been very fond of plenty of women in the past,' Kay said just as quietly as, the Voyager having driven out of sight, the twins disappeared up to their bedroom to reacquaint themselves with their room and toys as though they had been away for several months instead of several days.

'But how do you know this isn't different?'

'Because I face facts.' Kay turned to look at her mother once they had walked through into the kitchen to unpack the shopping Mitchell had insisted on paying for. 'For example, has Mitchell had other women back to the house for romantic dinners and so on in the past?'

Leonora wriggled uncomfortably. 'I guess so,' she admitted unhappily.

'You know so, and so do I. Probably quite a few stayed over too, and on a regular basis. They got to know Mitchell and be part of his life—but only for as long as he wanted them in it. That's the sort of man he is, Mum. He's head of a large and successful business, he works hard and plays hard, and enjoys the bachelor lifestyle with no ties and no commitments. All his loyalty and commitment is to his business.'

'That doesn't mean he couldn't give it to a woman if he fell in love,' Leonora argued stubbornly.

'That's a bigger ''if'' than you'll ever know where

Mitchell is concerned.' Leonora stared at her unhappily and Kay's voice softened as she said, 'Look, Mitchell doesn't understand about family. His own was disfunctional and violent, and he has never wanted to settle down. Why would he take on a ready-made family, for goodness' sake? And I come as a package, Mum. Those are the facts. Face them. I have.'

And then she surprised them both by bursting into tears. Some time later, after a mopping-up session followed by a hot, milky mug of chocolate, Leonora said apologetically, 'No more talking about you know who, I promise. Okay?'

Kay smiled. Until the next time. 'Okay. But don't let how things are with Mitchell and I affect your relationship with Henry, all right? He's lovely, I mean it, and I want you to see him as much as you want to. I think Mitchell and I will begin to tail off now, anyway, and it's all for the best. Really.' *Really.*

At ten o'clock Kay sat toasting her toes in front of the fire, a glass of wine at her elbow. Her mother had gone to bed early and she was all alone in the small sitting room, the Christmas tree lights twinkling and the beginnings of a storm howling outside, if the wind was anything to go by. It was cosy and snug, she was warm and safe with all her family around her—and she felt more miserable than she had ever felt in her life.

When the telephone rang she nearly jumped out of her skin, the book on her lap falling to the floor as she hastily reached for the receiver. 'Hallo?'

'Missing me?'

She nearly dropped the phone, her heart beginning to thunder. 'Mitchell?' she said weakly.

'I hope there's not another man in your life with the

right to ask you if you're missing him,' he said softly, his voice full of laughter. 'So, are you?'

'What?' Her brain wouldn't function.

'Missing me.'

'Are you missing me?' she prevaricated.

'Like hell.' There was no hesitation.

'Well, I'm missing you too.' What else could she say? she asked herself helplessly. Besides, it was the truth.

'Good.' She could tell he was smiling. 'Very good.'

There was a pause while Kay tried to steady her breathing and gain control of her rapid heartbeat. 'Where are you phoning from?' she asked quietly, hoping the trembling in her stomach didn't communicate itself to her voice.

'A hotel I use when I'm down here.' It was offhand and stated he didn't want to talk about his bed for the night.

'How were things when you arrived? As bad as you expected?'

'Worse.' She could hear the irritation in his voice as he thought of it and didn't envy the unfortunate Holden one little bit. 'Looks like I'll be a day or two at least trying to sort out the damn mess.' His voice changed. 'Think you can manage without me that long?' he asked softly.

'I'll just have to try, won't I?' she said lightly, having gained control of her equilibrium after the shock of hearing his voice.

'Don't try too hard.'

It wouldn't matter how hard she tried, she thought ruefully. He was the most fascinating man she had ever met—exciting, sexy, funny, handsome and she loved him to bits. She had never dreamt it was possible to be so captivated by another human being. So, all that being the case, what chance did she have of trying to squeeze him out of her life in a couple of days? It was going to take far, far longer than that, and buckets full of tears. 'You should be pleased I can manage without you,' she said levelly. 'No snares, no promises, right?'

'Modern woman.' There was a note in his voice she couldn't quite place and she wrinkled her nose as she tried to discern it.

'Exactly,' she agreed.

There was another pause. A second passed, then another and another. 'You can be too modern, you know,' he said with faint emphasis.

'I didn't know,' she said, still in a light tone. Keep it nice and easy, Kay, she thought as her heart raced.

'Neither did I until recently.'

She didn't know what to say or how to interpret the meaning of his words. Riddles, things half said, it was always the same. She never knew if she was on foot or horseback.

'How are the twins?' he asked in a different tone of voice entirely.

'Fine. Tired out. They spent ages arranging all the furniture in the doll's house after they'd decided where they wanted it in their bedroom. Big decision between on the floor next to the bookcase so they could lie on the carpet and play with it, or on the dressing table so they could sit on the stool. Georgia wanted the floor, Emily wanted the dressing table. I let them sort it out.'

'I bet I know who won,' he said wryly.

'No prizes, it was Georgia,' Kay admitted.

'She's nearly as strong-willed as her mother.' The smile in his voice softened any sting in the words.

Nevertheless, Kay felt compelled to protest, 'Strong will isn't a bad thing, surely?'

'No, unless...'

'Unless what?'

'It stops someone seeing what's under their nose.'

She blinked, completely taken aback.

'Goodnight, Kay,' he said smokily. 'Dream of me.'

This time she couldn't come back with the sarcasm she'd used the last time he had said the same words. She swallowed hard. 'Goodnight, Mitchell.'

She stood staring across the room with the telephone in her hands for some time after the line had gone dead, until it bleeped loudly at her. She replaced it slowly, her head spinning, and then reached for the glass of wine and drank the whole glassful straight down, whereupon she walked into the kitchen and poured herself another.

After reseating herself in front of the fire with the book on her lap again, she took another hefty sip of wine. If ever she needed a drink it was tonight, she thought ruefully. What was she going to do? Every time she made a conscious decision to withdraw it was as though he reached out and pulled her closer to him.

What did he want? Really want? With his strange, grim background and meteoric success, which had brought him wealth and power, what did he really want? Did he know himself? He had set the boundaries of their relationship in concrete at the beginning of it all, and he hadn't said anything specific to indicate he had changed. She would be crazy to hope that a few shrouded words and the odd glance might suggest she meant more to him than all the others. It wasn't even as if she had the sexual skills, the worldly knowledge, the sheer 'it' factor of his exes—not to mention the women he met socially and in business all the time.

Jealousy streaked through her and she clenched her stomach against it, telling herself not to be so stupid. She shut her eyes, relaxing into the plumpy back of the sofa.

He was in some anonymous hotel room right now—probably very luxurious, with everything he wanted at his fingertips, but characterless none the less. She wished she were with him; she wished it so much it was a physical ache in the essence of her.

CHAPTER TEN

MITCHELL wasn't due back until Monday some time, but he phoned Kay on Friday and Saturday night. Not for anything would she have admitted to a living soul that she was on tenterhooks all day long, every nerve and fibre in her body longing to hear his voice.

She'd got it bad, she told herself helplessly when, at three o'clock on Sunday morning, she still hadn't been able to drift off to sleep. And it scared her to death. Scared her witless, in fact. Which was what she was—witless, crazy, off her trolley, stark, staring and completely mad.

She sat up in bed, brushing her hair out of her eyes before throwing the duvet to one side and swinging her legs onto the floor. After reaching for her robe she slid her feet into her slippers and silently left the bedroom. Her mother was fast asleep; Leonora had spent the day with Henry and hadn't arrived home until gone eleven o'clock, whereupon Kay had noticed she was flushed and happy with the kind of rosy glow that suggested the day had gone extremely well.

Once downstairs she fixed herself a mug of hot milk sweetened with honey and carried it through into the sitting room, not bothering to turn on the light. There was a full moon slanting in through the windows and, with the glow of the dying fire in the grate, she could see enough.

She curled up on the sofa, cradling the warm mug as she sipped at the drink, and when it was finished she snuggled down, pulling her robe about her. Maybe she could sleep down here? she thought drowsily. She *was* tired, exhausted in fact, but for some reason the bedroom she had shared with her mother for the last few years had become claustrophobic the last day or two. Or perhaps it was just the fact that she had always been asleep as soon as her head touched the pillow in the past?

She must have fallen asleep because when the noise awoke her she was conscious of spiralling up from a deep, warm place where she'd been dreaming of Mitchell.

She was curled up in a little ball on the sofa in front of the now-dead fire and it still wasn't light, the moonlight causing dancing shadows to flicker across the room from the bare branches of the tree outside. Kay raised her head, peering over the back of the sofa towards the window as the noise—a kind of scratchy, fumbling sound—came again.

Afterwards she could never explain why she hadn't been frightened up to that point, but she hadn't. Maybe because the cat from across the way often prowled into their garden at night, or because she was still more asleep than awake, she didn't know, but in the same moment that a swirl of icy cold air met her face she saw the outlines of two men at the now-open window.

In the few seconds that she remained frozen with fear one of the men levered himself up onto the window sill, putting one leg into the room, and all the movements as silent as a cat.

The shrillness of Kay's scream, when it came, surprised even her, and after that several things seemed to happen all at the same time. She was aware of ducking down on the sofa and reaching for the poker in the grate, at the same time as she heard one of the men—the one inside the room, she thought—swear profusely and the other one say something urgently, although she couldn't work out what it was.

There was the sound of breaking glass, noise and scurry, but as the landing light went on and Leonora called, 'Kay? Kay, what's happening?' in a voice filled with terror, Kay knew they had gone.

'Stay with the girls,' she called urgently to her mother, rushing across to the light switch. 'I'm going to call the police. We've had some intruders.'

'Intruders? Oh, Kay, Kay! Are you hurt?' It sounded as though her mother was going into hysterics, but when the twins called from their bedroom Leonora's voice was more controlled as she answered, 'I'm coming, dears, don't worry. Everything's all right.'

'Keep them up there,' Kay warned as she dialled. 'I don't want them down here.' She was still gripping the poker and she knew she would have no compunction about using it should the men come back. 'I'm perfectly all right; they didn't touch me.'

In the few minutes in which it took the two young policemen to arrive, Kay stood by the phone without moving. She could see now the burglar who had been inside must have broken the window in his haste to escape, along with a heavy glass vase that had been on the window sill. She was shaking, her teeth chattering, as much from reaction as the freezing air swirling into the room.

They had been trying to invade her house, and with her babies asleep upstairs. She felt such a sickening mixture of shock and rage it made her legs tremble. *How dared they?*

When she heard the car draw up outside, she forced herself to walk to the front door and open it, her face ashen. The two policemen were wonderful, another car—this time with a female police officer—arriving moments later. While one of the policemen took a statement, the other searched the garden outside, but Kay had already told them she was sure the men had gone.

The woman police officer went upstairs to talk to Leonora, returning shortly and smiling at Kay as she said, 'You've got two lovely little girls.'

Yes, she had, and those men would have been here, in the same house with her precious babies. By rights she should have been asleep upstairs, Kay thought sickly. That was what they'd expected.

The police woman must have seen in her face what she was thinking because now she said briskly, 'A cup of tea, I think.'

It was a long night, but by the time a weak and windy dawn began to banish the darkness the police had gone through the wreckage with a fine-tooth comb, dusting and sorting and even finding a piece of glass with some blood on it.

'One of 'em cut themselves,' the policeman said with a great deal of satisfaction. 'Nice of 'em to leave a calling card. We might well find we've got this one on file.'

Her mother and the twins had come downstairs at some point, the children's curiosity overwhelming, but Kay was pleased and relieved to find both Georgia and Emily didn't really seem aware of the significance of what had happened. They had clung to her a while at first, and neat, tidy little Emily had been indignant about all the mess, but there had been no tears. It had been too cold for them to remain downstairs, and her mother had reported both girls were asleep within ten minutes or so once they'd been tucked up back in bed.

'Are you sure we can't call your brother or someone else, a friend maybe, before we leave, Mrs Sherwood?' the woman police officer had asked, once they had done all they could. One of the policemen had stuck a large piece of cardboard across the hole in the window, but the room was still icy.

Kay shook her head. 'No need to disturb anyone now,' she said quietly. It was still only seven o'clock. 'Time enough for that later.'

'I'm ringing Henry.' The police officers were hardly out of the door when Leonora picked up the telephone. 'He always rises at six and he'd want to know.'

More like her mother was longing to tell him, Kay thought indulgently. But she didn't mind. If she was honest her first coherent thought when she'd been waiting for the police to arrive had been an intense desire to be able to talk to Mitchell.

Her mother was a little deflated when the answer machine cut in after she had dialled the number, but, assuming Henry was down at the lake feeding the ducks their normal hearty breakfast, she left a message and hung up.

Once Kay had showered and dressed she felt better, although the white face staring back at her from the mirror still looked like death warmed up. Coffee. Lots of strong, sweet coffee before the girls woke up, she thought practically. Those men, whoever they were, weren't going to get the better of her. She wouldn't let them frighten her, not in her own house.

She put the coffee on to percolate while her mother went upstairs to wash and dress, and was just checking every tiny piece of glass had gone when she heard a car screech to a halt outside. Henry, bless him. He'd obviously heard her mother's message and come flying over in person, rather than ringing back.

She got up from her knees and walked to the front door. They had closed the curtains earlier, hoping it would help to warm the room a little, but it was still icy cold, despite the heating being on. She didn't wait for Henry to knock, opening the door with a smile of welcome, which remained fixed in surprise when she found herself looking into a pair of silver-blue eyes set in an ominously dark face as Mitchell strode up the path, Henry following some yards behind.

'Are you all right?' He didn't wait for her to speak, taking her into his arms as he reached her and holding her so tight she couldn't breathe. 'I'll tear them limb from limb, I swear it.'

'Mitchell, *Mitchell*.' She had to struggle to become free, but when she saw the look on his face her voice gentled. 'I'm fine, I am,' she said quickly. 'No one was hurt—no one but one of the burglars, anyway.'

She had stepped backwards into the sitting room as she'd spoken, the two men following her, but as Henry shut the door Mitchell pulled her to him again, his voice hoarse as he murmured, 'I'd have killed them if they'd hurt a hair on your head. Damn it, I should have *been* here.'

She understood immediately. Her hand lifted to his face and he grabbed it and held it there as she said, 'No, you shouldn't, of course you shouldn't. You can't be everywhere,' knowing that old ghosts had been resurrected and the torment of his sister's death was heavy on his shoulders.

Henry was standing silently behind them, his face grim, and now Kay said, 'Mum's getting dressed, Henry, but there's coffee on the go in the kitchen if you'd like to take charge. And don't you look like that either—we really are all right.'

'Kay, Kay...' As Henry disappeared into the other room Mitchell's hands moved to cradle her face, his lips desperate as they bruised hers in an agony of fear at what might have been. 'Are the twins okay? How badly were they frightened?'

She loved that he'd thought of the girls. 'They're too young to really realise what's happened,' she said softly, her lips tingling and burning. 'I'm not sure how they'll be today, but they're still asleep so that's a good sign.'

'When I think what could have happened—'

'Don't.' She cut off his voice by putting a finger to his lips. 'The police think they are just two petty thieves who have been working this area, apparently. They break in at night and go for things like the TV and video, but they're not violent. One of them cut themselves on the window, they were so desperate to get away when I screamed.'

'You screamed?' His face went greyer. 'Damn it, Kay, I want to do murder.'

Kay thought he needed a cup of coffee more than she did. She pulled him over to the sofa and when they were both sitting down, his arm enclosing her, she said, after they had kissed again, 'What are you doing here? I didn't think you got back until this afternoon?'

'I worked through the night and made the others do the same,' he said grimly, 'and caught the early train this morning. Henry was collecting me from the station when your mother called.'

'You worked through the night? Why?'

'Because I wanted to see you as soon as possible,' he said simply.

Her heart leapt and then began to pound.

'We need to talk, Kay. I can't go on like this,' he said softly, 'but now is not the time. Later.'

She stared at him, doubt mixing with exhilaration. Was this his way of telling her she had to make a decision about the future? Accept his terms or else? The 'iron fist in the velvet glove' approach? She didn't know; she just didn't know. How could you ever read Mitchell's mind?

'Tell me exactly what happened here, Kay,' he said quietly as Henry appeared from the kitchen with a tray holding the coffee. 'Minute by minute.'

Her mother appeared at the top of the stairs just as she began to relate the story, and Kay was left in no doubt as to Henry's feelings for her mother—or her mother's for Henry, come to that—by the exchange between the couple.

Once they were all sitting down, Kay told the two men everything that had happened before they transferred to the kitchen for toast and marmalade and more coffee.

Kay was beginning to feel panicky about what was to come. Mitchell was thoroughly in control of himself again, his brief glitch when he'd first arrived gone as completely as if it had never happened at all. He was attentive, considerate, but his eyes were veiled against her and his face was giving nothing away. She knew all over again that she just didn't understand what made him tick. But he had come, she told herself feverishly. He had rushed here to her side when he'd thought she needed him. That had to mean something, didn't it?

Guilt? a nasty little voice in her head said tauntingly. Could it mean guilt? He had never got over the way he felt he had let his sister down; perhaps this morning hadn't really been about her, Kay Sherwood, so much as demons from the past?

The four of them were still sitting talking when Georgia and Emily came padding downstairs, the little girls' transparent delight at seeing Mitchell causing Kay further misgivings. They adored him, she told herself helplessly as she watched the girls clamber onto his lap. And he was so good with them.

It was mid-morning when Mitchell rose to his feet and took Kay's hand. 'Go and get your coat,' he said quietly. 'We're going for a drive and lunch somewhere after I've phoned a guy I know to come and fix the window.'

'It's a Sunday.' Kay stared at him in surprise. 'No one works on a Sunday.'

'He'll come.' Mitchell turned to Henry and Leonora. 'You two okay to hold the fort for a while?'

'Of course,' said Leonora eagerly, too eagerly, clearly delighted by events.

'Can we come?' Georgia asked immediately.

'Not this time, honey, okay? But I promise we'll go somewhere nice soon,' Mitchell said gently.

'Can we see the ducks again?'

This was obviously considered the ultimate in nice. Mitchell smiled, ruffling the small head of curls as he said, 'I don't see why not.'

Oh, please, God, make all this turn out right, Kay prayed as she fetched her coat, not even stopping to check her hair or put any make-up on. If I'm not what he wants, if he can't break free of the past, don't let my girls be hurt.

As they walked towards the car Mitchell took her hand and Kay found she couldn't speak at all, but her fingers wound themselves round his. She felt in her bones what he was going to say would either make or break them, and she didn't have any idea which way it would go.

'I've finished racing at the circuit.'

It was the very last thing in all the world she had expected him to say, and now, as she slid into the car, she stared up at him as he stood holding the door open for her.

'For good?' she asked after a moment or two.

'Oh, yes, Kay, for good.'

She nodded, her heart beginning to thud harder. 'I'm glad.'

'I'm glad you're glad.'

'Mitchell—'

'Not yet, Kay. I want to talk to you, really talk to you somewhere quiet where there's just the two of us.' He shut the door, walking round the bonnet and climbing into the driver's seat. 'There's a pub I know that serves excellent Sunday lunch not too far from here and you don't have to book.' He glanced at her, his eyes crystal-clear. 'We can be there by twelve after I've said what I need to say first.'

Kay nodded. 'Fine.' Fine? What a stupid thing to say when she was so nervous she knew she would never be able to eat again in the whole of her life.

He drove out of the town and into the country and he didn't say a word as the powerful car ate up the miles. They had been travelling for about twenty minutes when he pulled off the road and into a gateway that overlooked a valley still white with snow. It was beautiful, tranquil and sweepingly majestic, the trees stark and bare against the pale world surrounding them. A few lone birds were flying overhead but otherwise everything was still, a frozen world captured in time.

She sat staring straight ahead for a moment as the engine died, and then she forced herself to turn her head and look at him, knowing he was staring intently at her.

She saw a muscle clench in his jaw as he looked into her eyes. 'We both said a lot of things when we first met.' He said quietly. 'Do you remember?'

Did she remember? They had haunted her ever since. 'What sort of things?' she murmured warily, still terribly unsure of where he was coming from.

He gave a short, mirthless laugh. 'Stupid things.' He

raked back his hair, the action impatient but at the same time carrying a hint of nervousness. 'And yet not so stupid because I thought that was how I felt at the time, that I would never—' He stopped abruptly. 'What I mean is, until then—'

He paused again and Kay stared at him in disbelief. Mitchell, controlled, concise Mitchell, ruthless and focused and as to the point as a sharp blade, struggling for words? Somehow it was more illuminating than anything that had happened that morning.

'What are you trying to say?' she whispered weakly, knowing it had to come from him. If what she was daring to hope was true, it had to start now, properly, for it to have any chance at all.

'I love you, Kay,' he said grimly.

She looked at him, a tiny part of her mind that seemed to be working separately from the rest of her pointing out that even in declaring himself Mitchell had to be different from other men. He had spoken more as though he were pronouncing a death sentence on her, rather than giving her the one thing in all the world she really wanted.

'I know you don't feel the same, not yet, and I can understand that,' he said quickly as she remained stock-still just staring at him, her mind racing as she still didn't dare let the hope run free. 'But one of the things we said when we first met was that if either party wanted the situation to change, one way or the other, they had to say. Well, I'm saying, Kay. I've had a bellyful of going softly, softly, and this last episode with those ba—' he stopped short, taking a deep breath before he continued '—with those men this morning was the final straw. I need you to know how I feel. I need to be able to have the right to strangle scum like those two because they dared to come anywhere near the woman of my heart,' he finished angrily.

Kay stared at his dark, furious face and thought she had never loved him so much as in this moment.

'Kay, I want a future for us,' he continued with barely a pause, his chest rising and falling with the force of his emotion. 'I want—oh, I want the lot, I guess. But I won't rush you, I'll keep to that—' And then, as though to disprove the last words, he said, 'Say something, damn it.'

Oh, Mitchell. She swallowed, fighting back the tears as she said, 'You...you're sure? I mean, really sure? There's the girls...'

'More sure than I've ever been of anything in the whole of my life.' He was looking at her intently now, his face changing as he took in her trembling mouth. 'I want you in my life for ever, I want a ring on your finger to keep the other wolves off and to let them know that you are mine. Is that chauvinistic?'

'Probably.' Tears had spilled out of her eyes now but she smiled tremulously.

He reached out a wondering hand and touched a glittering tear as it hung on an eyelash. 'Does this mean you care a little?' he asked shakily.

He looked big and dark and handsome as he sat looking at her uncertainly, his jet-black hair in stark contrast to the piercing silvery-blue eyes, and she wondered what she had ever done to deserve the love of this man. Because it was there, shining in his eyes. He was letting her see it and it filled her heart with such joy she could hardly breathe.

'I've loved you for the whole of my life,' she whispered, 'long before I knew you. When I first saw you, something happened inside and it scared me to death. I tried to tell myself it was all sorts of things but it grew and grew and finally I had to admit it was love. A for-ever love. But you didn't want me like that...'

'Oh, my love, my love.' His voice was thick as he took her into his arms, pulling her against the wall of his chest as he nuzzled into her hair.

'I tried not to fall in love with you, so hard, but it happened right from the first,' she said, her voice muffled against his overcoat. 'But you had had so many women, beautiful women.'

'I never loved one of them.' His voice was soft above her head. 'I liked some more than others but they never stirred my heart. If I'm honest, until I met you I didn't want to acknowledge there could be anything beyond sexual attraction between a man and a woman and I didn't have to. Then you came along, and...'

He hesitated, and she said, 'Yes? Tell me,' as she raised her head, kissing the corner of his hard mouth, still unable to believe she could do that freely now.

'I had always told myself that my father didn't love my mother towards the end, that she had burnt his love out,' he said huskily, the words being forced up from some dark place within him. 'It was the only way I could come to terms with an essentially good man like he was loving a woman like her. I told myself he stayed with her because he believed in family, that misguidedly he thought having a father *and* mother was more important than splitting us up. But deep down I knew it wasn't true, and that's what I've been fighting ever since the accident. He still loved her, Kay. He sacrificed my sister—he would have sacri-ficed anyone—to be with her, to hang onto her. I never wanted any woman to have that sort of power over me. It filled me with abhorrence, with disgust, but mostly blind fear.'

He looked down at her, his mouth twisting. 'Great, eh? I'm a mess, I admit it.'

'I'll sort you out.' She smiled up at him, her arms going tight round his neck. 'I promise.'

'I believe you can.' His voice held a note of wonder.

'We can do anything, the two of us,' she said, happy tears still squeezing themselves out of her eyes. 'We can take on the whole world and win.'

'I only want you,' he said huskily. 'When you told me how badly you'd been let down, how you'd fought back, taking on the responsibility of your mother and the business, even sorting your brother's life out, I couldn't believe that a tiny, slim little scrap like you could have that sort of fire and will-power in her. Boy, did I learn fast,' he added wryly. 'And more surprises were in store. I met your daughters. *Daughters*. And you not looking old enough to be out of pigtails at times.'

He pulled her into him again, kissing away the tears and then taking her mouth in a kiss that shook her to her very roots. His breathing was heavy when at last he lifted his head, his lips slowly leaving hers.

'The twins, Mitchell. You don't mind that they come with me?' she whispered, feeling she knew the answer but needing to hear it all the same.

'Mind?' He kissed her again. 'Oh, my darling, how could I mind? They're wonderful, amazing, two miniature Kays. Georgia has all of your determination and fire, and little Emily is your other side, the vulnerable, needing reassurance, unsure part of you. Two little individual clones from one beautiful lady.'

'They love you already.' Her hand moved gently to his mouth again, her fingers tracing his lips. 'Children see so much more clearly than us at times. They recognised the real Mitchell long before you let me see him.'

'I think your mother is for me too,' he said with some satisfaction, grinning down at her suddenly. 'I sensed an ally in her from the very beginning.'

'As well you might.' She met his eyes in amusement.

'Marry me, Kay.'

His voice was soft with a catch in it and her heart soared with the birds overhead. 'Yes,' she said shakily, 'but not straight away. First we'll get the twins used to the idea and just have some time...'

She didn't know how to put it, and he finished for her, his face understanding, 'Getting used to it ourselves?'

Did he know there was still just the tiniest doubt, the merest smidgen that he might find he couldn't do the whole family thing? She didn't know, but she was grateful he had put it the way he had. She nodded. 'I love you, Mitchell, with all my heart,' she said before she pulled his head down to hers.

Just so that he knew.

CHAPTER ELEVEN

'Do I look all right, Kay? Are you sure this suit is my colour?'

'Mum, you look fantastic. When you walk up the aisle Henry is going to be knocked sideways,' Kay said reassuringly as she looked into her mother's flushed, anxious face.

It was true—Leonora did look amazing in the pale cream suit and huge bridal hat with pale blue feathers waving gently over the rim.

'Is the car here yet?'

Leonora was flapping, but then every bride had the right to be nervous on her wedding day. Kay smiled at her mother, putting out a hand and touching Leonora's dear face before she said gently, 'Everything's under control, Mum. And if I hear correctly, I think the car's just arrived.'

She hung out of the bedroom window of Ivy Cottage and, sure enough, an elegant cream Rolls complete with ribbons and driver was waiting outside, its paintwork shining in the mild December sunshine.

Leonora turned to her daughter, her voice trembling as she said, 'The end of an era, Kay.'

'And a great new one about to start.'

'Your father wouldn't have minded me marrying again, would he?'

'Of course he wouldn't.' Kay took her mother into her arms, mindful of the new hat. 'And it isn't as if you've exactly rushed into it, is it? Two years you've kept that

180

poor man waiting; it's about time you made an honest man of him.'

'Oh, Kay.' Leonora giggled and then took a deep breath. 'Right, I'm ready.'

The drive to the church through the slanting sunshine was very pleasant, but Leonora kept tight hold of Kay's hand all the time. Kay could understand why. Her mother had had her own gremlins to come to terms with before she had felt she could finally commit to Henry. Kay's father had been a good man and they had been happy most of the time, but it wasn't until Henry had proposed to her mother some months after Mitchell had popped the question that Kay had realised how the past had affected Leonora. The uncertainty about money, which had been a constant thorn in Leonora's flesh when she had been married before, the final catastrophic finale when she had been left with nothing due to Kay's father's speculating, had all taken its toll.

But Henry's persistence had finally paid off. He wanted her as his wife, he had insisted firmly. Not as his companion or his partner or any other of the modern terms bandied about these days. He was old-fashioned, he admitted it, but he wanted a gold ring on the third finger of Leonora's left hand and that was that.

'I've never really said thank you for saving me after your father died,' Leonora said quietly as the church came in sight.

'Saving you?' Kay stared at her mother. 'I didn't save you.'

'Oh, yes, you did, darling.' Leonora squeezed her daughter's hand. 'I was in a state, more of a state than I was willing to admit to anyone at the time. You left a secure job, a flat, all that you'd worked for for yourself and the twins after Perry left, and you came home to be with me. And you did it so sweetly. Never once did you make me feel as if you didn't want to be there.'

'I did want to be there, that's why,' Kay said softly, smiling at her mother as she added, 'And don't cry, not now, not when I've done your make-up so well.'

'Even my meeting Henry was through you.' Leonora gave a loud sniff and then put down the little winter posy she was carrying. 'Have you got a tissue, darling?'

'Oh, Mum.' Kay grinned at her mother. 'I do love you.'

'And I love you.'

Then the car stopped at the little wicker gate in front of the long, winding path leading to the church door, and it was all flurry and movement for a minute as Kay helped her mother out, adjusting her hat and handing her the posy once she was on the pavement.

'Grandma! Grandma!' The twins had been waiting just inside the gate, holding Mitchell's hands, and now they came dancing out, small faces aglow as they caught sight of Leonora and their mother.

Kay smiled at her husband.

They had married within six months of his proposal, a quiet summer wedding with just family present and the girls as bridesmaids, dressed in fairy-tale dresses of white muslin and pink rosebuds. It had been wonderful, magical.

Now the twins were being bridesmaids again, but this time they were in blue satin with fake fur muffs and little warm cloaks. Her mother—the most conventional of women normally—had cut with protocol and insisted she wanted Kay to give her away, and with Mitchell being Henry's best man it was a real family affair.

Kay looked at her husband now as he hurried up the church path to take his place beside Henry, ready for when they came in. She touched the round mound of her stomach briefly wherein their first child, a little boy

with strong, healthy limbs, from what the scan had revealed, lay.

Mitchell had cried with joy when he had seen his son
on the monitor; in fact he'd had them all crying—the doctor and herself as much with the look on his face as the
wonder of the new little life growing inside her.

And it had happened at just the right time. With Henry
now leaving their house to live with her mother in Ivy
Cottage, and Kay just having finished work completely
after making the delivery business over to Peter, lock,
stock and barrel, she felt ready to become a housewife
again.

It had taken a little time for her to be comfortable with
the idea after she had fought so hard for a measure of
independence with Perry, but life was so different with
Mitchell, so absolutely wonderful and perfect and glori-
ous, that all her faint doubts had disappeared. He loved
her in a way she had never dreamt of being loved, only
desiring the best for her, and she felt more treasured and
cherished than any woman on earth.

'"Perfect love casteth out fear." She murmured the
words the minister had spoken on her wedding day, and
which had stayed with her ever since.

'What was that, dear?'

Her mother had turned to her, and now Kay said as she
pushed open the gate, 'Nothing, Mum. Come on, he's
waiting.'

They walked up the long path hand in hand, and when
the wedding march sounded and Kay had ushered Georgia
and Emily in front of them they still walked hand in hand
to Henry and Mitchell, waiting at the end of the aisle.

The sunlight had turned the stained-glass window overlooking the altar into a spectacular backdrop, and as Kay

delivered her mother into Henry's care and took her place in the front pew her heart was full.

She loved the most wonderful man in all the world and he loved her. Their days were filled with warmth and closeness, Mitchell hungry for all that real family life meant, but it was the nights, when it was just the two of them in their huge, soft bed, that she felt she really became the woman she'd always been destined to be.

In the warm afterglow of their lovemaking, lovemaking that was so wonderful and incredible that sometimes she thought she would die from the pleasure he induced, he would tell her how much he loved her. She was his woman, his treasure, his reason for breathing, the only woman in the world for him—beautiful, perfect and incomparably precious.

And in the soft darkness she would hold him close, her body moulded into his as she laid her heart and her soul bare before him. She kept nothing back; she didn't have to. He was Mitchell, her husband, and she could trust him completely, and she wanted to give him the reassurance she knew he would always need. The world saw a strong, powerful, ruthless man, but that was only a part of him. The real part, *her part*, was so much more than that.

As he joined her in the pew Mitchell smiled at her. 'Happy, love?' he asked softly, his fingers brushing over his child briefly as his eyes devoured her in a most unchurchlike way.

'More than I can say,' she answered mistily as joy and gratitude for all that life held flooded her heart. Life was rich and filled with love. She had Mitchell, she had her family and there was new, strong life growing inside her.

She was blessed.

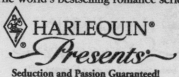

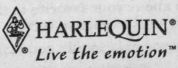

If you enjoyed what you just read,
then we've got an offer you can't resist!

Take 2 bestselling
love stories FREE!

Plus get a FREE surprise gift!

The men and women of California's
Courage Bay Emergency Services team
must face any emergency...even the
ones that are no accident!

CODE RED

Coming in December...

BLOWN AWAY

by
MURIEL JENSEN

Being rescued by gorgeous K-9 Officer
Cole Winslow is a fantasy come true for
single mom Kara Abbott. But, despite
their mutual attraction, Kara senses
Cole is holding back. Now it's Kara's
turn to rescue Cole—from the grip
of his past.

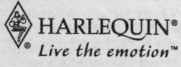

The world's bestselling romance series.

Seduction and Passion Guaranteed!

Looking for stories that sizzle?

Wanting a read that has a little extra spice?

Harlequin Presents® is thrilled to bring you romances that turn up the heat!

Don't miss...

AT THE SPANISH DUKE'S COMMAND

by bestselling MIRA® author
Fiona Hood-Stewart

On sale February 2005, #2448

**Pick up a PRESENTS PASSION™ novel—
where seduction is guaranteed!**

Available wherever Harlequin books are sold.

The world's bestselling romance series.

HARLEQUIN®

Presents~

Seduction and Passion Guaranteed!

Back by popular demand...

EXPECTING!

She's sexy,
successful and
PREGNANT!

Relax and enjoy our fabulous series about
couples whose passion results in pregnancies...
sometimes unexpected!

Share the surprises, emotions, drama and suspense
as our parents-to-be come to terms with the prospect
of bringing a new life into the world. All will
discover that the business of making babies brings
with it the most special love of all....

Our next arrival will be

HIS PREGNANCY BARGAIN by *Kim Lawrence*
On sale January 2005, #2441
Don't miss it!

THE BRABANTI BABY by *Catherine Spencer*
On sale February 2005, #2450

www.eHarlequin.com   HPEXP0105